Roscoe Conkling

Argument of Hon. Roscoe Conkling, June 26, 1866

before a special committee of the House of representatives, raised to

investigate the administration of the Bureau of the provost marshal

general

Roscoe Conkling

Argument of Hon. Roscoe Conkling, June 26, 1866
before a special committee of the House of representatives, raised to investigate the administration of the Bureau of the provost marshal general

ISBN/EAN: 9783337380991

Printed in Europe, USA, Canada, Australia, Japan

Cover: Foto ©Andreas Hilbeck / pixelio.de

More available books at **www.hansebooks.com**

ARGUMENT

OF

HON. ROSCOE CONKLING,

JUNE 26, 1866,

Before a Special Committee of the House of Representatives, raised to investigate the administration of the Bureau of the Provost Marshal General, and also the act of James B. Fry, the head of the said bureau, in sending to the House a letter libelling the character of one of its members, and also the truth of said letter.

Mr. CHAIRMAN AND GENTLEMEN OF THE COMMITTEE : Before proceeding to the argument itself, I wish to remind you of the circumstances out of which this investigation grew. On the 24th of April the House of Representatives had under consideration the "Army bill." The Military Committee had been induced to adopt a section rendering the office and bureau of the Provost Marshal General perpetual—transforming it from a temporary invention of the war into a permanent element of the peace establishment. A motion was made by me to strike out this section, and my reasons for the motion were given in the House at the time. In assigning these reasons I reviewed the public administration of an executive officer, and the management of the bureau of which he was the head.

As a part of my remarks, I caused to be read a letter from the Lieutenant General of the army, which letter had been addressed and sent to a member of the Military Committee of the Senate, and had been used as evidence and information against the proposition to continue by legislation the office of Provost Marshal General. This letter was called out by a communication addressed to the Lieutenant General by a member of the Senate committee, and had been sent to me to be used in debate in the House of Representatives.

In reply to the motion made by me, and to the remarks submitted in support of that motion, and to the letter in question, a member of the House, Mr. Blaine, made a personal attack on me. He charged that the letter of the Lieutenant General had been improperly brought into the House by me. The term he used was, "smuggled in," and, having uttered this imputation, he proceeded further to arraign my motives. He charged that I had had "quarrels" with General Fry; he charged that in these "quarrels" I "came out second best at the War Department." He charged that I had traduced General Fry, and had done so in his absence, and in a place where he could not be heard. In a subsequent portion of his remarks he said that he understood there were "personal difficulties" between myself and General Fry; and, speaking of General Fry, he used the following words: "And he is ready to meet the gentleman from New York, and all other accusers, anywhere and everywhere."

In answer to these personal and offensive remarks, I pronounced them false, and, denying all intention to confine the statement of my opinion and knowledge of General Fry's administration to a place where General Fry could not be heard, I stated that I was ready to make my statements good wherever the question of their correctness might be raised. The House, by an almost unanimous vote, sustained the motion to discard the office of Provost Marshal General.

...ay here remind the committee that to pro_ounce "... ...... a statement, 'or
...n the report of a committee, is the right of a member of a parliamentary body,
...d in doing so, he does not transgress the limits established by parliamentary
practice, the distinction being between imputing an intentional falsehood to
another, and pronouncing false a statement itself. This distinction is especially
palpable in a case where the statement made is of such a nature as to show
upon its face that it does not originate with the member who utters it, but de-
pends for its truth upon the statement given him by some third person.

On the 30th of April, six days after the proceedings referred to, General Fry
sent, and Mr. Blaine brought into the House and caused to be read, a lengthy
letter, accompanied by various exhibits and documents formally certified. This
letter contains an elaborate and studied libel, or rather a long series of libels,
upon my private character, the undisguised purpose being to inflict injury upon
me in retaliation for words spoken in debate.

The House, in vindication of its own honor, ordered, at my suggestion, an investigation, not only of the administration of the Provost Marshal General and
his bureau, but also of the act of sending the letter in 'question, and of the
contents of that letter. The committee in entering upon its duties resolved
that before proceeding to investigate the official conduct of General Fry at
large, they would first of all investigate his act in sending a libel into the House
of Representatives in revenge upon a member for words spoken and votes
given in the House. This inquiry involved the truth of that libel, and the
motives with which it was written and sent. In one sense such an inquiry
may be deemed personal, and in so far it is narrow and unimportant, but in the
true sense, the inquiry is broad and important, and not confined to the interest of
any individual.

The right to speak freely in debate and to vote without interference, while it
is the right of the representative, is still more the right of every constituency.
It is the great right of the people, and as such has ever been cherished in every
system of free government. In England it has been maintained for centuries
as the supreme prerogative and privilege of the public. And our fathers, in lay-
ing the foundations of government, jealously preserved in the spirit and letter
of the institutions they formed, the same absolute exemption. Since the Constitution was adopted nearly a century has elapsed, and never until now has so
audacious and offensive an attempt been made to strike a senator or representative in his private character in revenge for acts done officially. It is submitted
that a more enormous breach of privilege can scarcely be conceived of. A man
who out of the House commits a bodily assault upon a member is held guilty of
a high offence. A man who should go into the presence of the House and during its session should commit an act of personal violence upon a member,
would be held to have defiled all the sanctities of the place, trampled upon the
rights of the body, and struck at the very principle of its existence; and yet
will any one affirm, looking to the private or the public wrong attempted, that
a bodily injury of such a kind is greater in criminality or extent than the act
of a man who sends into the House, to be read in its face, and published to the
world, a reeking malignant attack upon the personal character and official reputation of one or more of its members.?

The assailant in this case is a military officer, a man bound by official obligations and invested with official advantages. He is bound by an oath of office
to support the government in all its branches, and to maintain the Constitution.
On the other hand, he has opportunities insured to him, which are denied to
citizens at large, of vindicating himself from injustice or misconstruction as to
his official acts. If wrong was done him in the criticisms made upon his administration, it was his privilege to demand a court of inquiry, or to invite a court-
martial, and thus to create for himself a tribunal composed of men of his own
profession, and certain to be, at least, impartial towards him. It was his right

so to ask a congressional investigation. Either of these courses would have indicated General Fry, if, in truth, he had been innocent. Indeed either of tem would have secured his acquittal had there been a reasonable doubt of his uilt; but in place of resorting to any proper and lawful means of vindication : defence, he chose to obtain or accept the connivance of a member of the House, id through him to make a foul attack upon the character of another member hom he held responsible, in part at least, for the rejection of his bureau, id for the debate which occurred at the time. There can be no pretence that ic letter in question was designed as a plea in self-defence. The only allusions tade to any matters tending to the vindication of General Fry are incidental id subordinate, its whole aim and purpose being to blacken the character of ic person assailed and to spread its imputation beyond the reach of counter :tion. All this would be true even if the statements of General Fry were)unded in fact, or if they had been by him believed to be true. But the case aggravated by reason of the wantonness, the bad faith, and the malevolence y which the writer was prompted. Six weeks have been spent by General Fry i an effort to hunt up or invent something from which the committee might ifer that he believed what he said; but despite all these endeavors the fact is alpable as to every substantial statement of his letter that he neither believed cr suspected it to be true, but knew it to be false when he made it.

I shall endeavor to show by the evidence, with equal certainty, that the mo-ve of General Fry was base and malicious beyond the baseness and malice ·hich ordinarily prompt the utterance of injurious falsehoods, and, therefore, for ie purposes of this argument, I assume the position and undertake the task of show-ig affirmatively, item by item, the untruthfulness and malice of General Fry. have preferred not to leave the matter in any of its parts to stand upon the iere absence of evidence to uphold it. I have preferred not to avail myself of ny presumptions which the law raises against unproved slanders, and I have vailed myself of the broadest permission the committee would give, to introduce ffirmative evidence. This permission has been a narrow one. The committee iled that upon this branch of the investigation, no evidence would be received xcept that bearing directly upon the motive with which the letter was written, r upon the truth or falsity of the statements in the letter bearing directly upon ic. Notwithstanding the taut rein thus held, enough evidence has been re-:ived to show General Fry guilty not only of falsehood and dishonor as a man; uilty not only of the most cowardly slander; guilty not only of violating his ffic'al oath; guilty not only of breaking the rules, violating the regulations, and ·ampling upon the most cherished virtue of his profession, but guilty also of ich official malfeasance as closes the door of charity and credulity against all xtenuation.

In order to determine how far I have warrant for these allegations, I proceed ow to review and examine the evidence. Let us begin with the first substan-ul statement made by General Fry. He says: "I am enabled to say that your ssertions touching Mr. Conkling's difficulties with this bureau are amply and ompletely justified by the facts which this letter will disclose."

These words contain an imputation of falsehood, as do other subsequent 'ords in the letter relating to the same subject. I shall not forget to recur to iem again, and show the committee their effrontery and groundlessness. But ir convenience I will pass them now, and consider them with the subsequent arts of the letter with which they belong. The next passage in the letter is iis:

"My official intercourse with representatives in Congress during the past irce years has been constant, and in many cases intimate, and, with the soli-iry exception of Mr. Conkling, it has been marked, so far as I remember, by iutual honor and fair dealing. Mr. Conkling being thus an exception, it is my purpose to give a brief summary of his connexion and intercourse with this bureau"

I offered to prove by different members of Congress the total falsehood of this statement. I offered to show that the intercourse of General Fry with other representatives in Congress had been unfair and dishonorable, his conduct insolent, and his language profane, and that he had been denounced to himself as a dishonored man. This the committee excluded because it overthrew that part of the statement which had no reference to me. But beside this portion of it, there is a distinct suggestion that there has been dishonorable and unfair dealing on my part with General Fry; and availing myself of the opportunity, evidence has been given to show that, in all the intercourse between the Provost Marshal bureau and myself, nothing has occurred to justify or extenuate this statement. On the other hand, General Fry has offered no evidence tending in any way to explain or excuse the imputation, much less to prove it, and leaving the committee to pronounce upon it, I pass to other matters.

The next allegation of General Fry is in these words:

"In the summer of 1863 Mr. Conkling made a case for himself by telegraphing to the War Department that the provost marshal of his district required *legal advice,* which he was thereupon empowered to give."

This stands as the first specification in the charge of unfair dealing with the Provost Marshal General. The circumstance to which reference is made has been detailed to the committee by Judge Hunt and other witnesses. These facts disprove the allegation; but if that were all, room would be left to suppose that General Fry made his statement under some misapprehension. The attention of the committee is, therefore, invited to the question, whether there can have been an honest mistake on this subject. Unless General Fry had something upon which he relied in making his statement, his assertion was certainly dishonorable. If he had no knowledge or information one way or another, he would be wholly indefensible, however the truth might be. It is material, therefore, to inquire whether he had ever heard or seen any statement to bear out his accusation. He offers no proof of any. He omits and refuses himself to testify to any; and the proof before the committee demonstrates that he had full knowledge of the truth, and that he purposely misstated it. Indeed, this passage is one of the most frigid, premeditated falsehoods in a column of wilful misstatements. The occurrence referred to was somewhat old and far-fetched. It had evidently been hunted up. It was hunted up, perhaps, as long ago as the commencement of the session, when a resolution was offered by me inquiring into the necessity of prolonging the Provost Marshal's bureau. Mr. Stanton, it will be remembered, said that General Fry asked him a long time ago whether he had any objection to his making a defence of himself; and the age of the circumstance in question, and its remoteness from anything brought in question in the House with regard to General Fry, raises a strong presumption that it had been looked up with malice aforethought. The mode of stating it also shows that the despatches had been referred to. The time is given as the summer of 1863. It is stated that the communication was by telegraph, and various ear-marks show that the telegram was within the knowledge of the writer at the date of the letter. Yet that telegram, proved as it is to be literally true in all its statements, shows a reckless violation of truth by General Fry. It shows that I did not "make a case for myself," and it shows that I did not telegraph that the provost marshal, or any other person, needed "legal advice;" but simply that I communicated facts of an important nature, and recommended that the officers of the government should be directed from Washington as to the action they should take.

The evidence discloses that the representative of the district at the time, Mr. Kernan, could not be called on to confer with the authorities at Washington, as he was the counsel conducting the proceedings against the government officers who had arrested and held the alleged deserter; that the officers had in vain sought instruction and advice; that an attachment was in the hands of the sheriff to compel the provost marshal to produce his prisoner, which he refused to do; and that the time, the occasion, and the circumstances were such as to disturb the community with the fear of forcible collision between the State and national authorities.

Having been the representative of the district, I was asked to communicate the facts to the government at Washington, and I did so by a communication prepared in the presence of many persons. This was my whole action in the matter.

The facts were well known to General Fry at the time. This clearly appears, because the answer to my communication has been produced, and is from General Fry himself, and we find him afterwards writing a letter about the same matter, and making requests in regard to it.

Yet, in defiance of all the facts, this obvious and blameless occurrence is trumped up, and an infamous insinuation put forth in regard to it.

The comment which this part of the letter of General Fry deserves is left to the committee.

I ask you now to consider the next passage, which is as follows:

"In April, 1865, Mr. Charles A. Dana, then Assistant Secretary of War, without notifying me, had Mr. Conkling appointed to investigate all frauds in enlistments in western New York, with the stipulation that he should be commissioned judge advocate for the prosecution of any cases brought to trial, and he was so appointed to prosecute before a general court-martial Major J. A. Haddock. Mr. Dana vested him, by several orders issued in the name of the Secretary of War, without the sanction of Mr. Stanton, with the most extraordinary powers."

I propose to examine this piecemeal. First. "*Without notifying me.*" These words, bursting with self-importance, are also full of untruth. The transaction to which they refer took place, as the papers show, on Monday, April 3, 1865, and the proof is conclusive that on the same day, and early in the day, and as soon as the matter occurred, it was fully communicated to General Fry. The subject was first broached the day previous, April 2. On that day the Secretary of War proposed the matter, and it was discussed and held under consideration, and even this, on the same day that it occurred and before any conclusion had been reached, was communicated to General Fry, and was known to him from his own observation also. Mr. Stanton and Mr. Dana both prove this positively. Who denies it? Does General Fry dare testify that he had forgotten it when he asserted to the contrary?

One of the counsel, while in actual consultation with his client during Mr. Dana's examination, put leading questions to show that the papers relating to Haddock and his alleged crimes, were sent for on the 2d of April to be submitted to me, and that General Fry was sent for in person also, and came in and saw the papers actually undergoing examination. They seemed to forget that, while thus pursuing some other point in the case, they were uncovering the fact that General Fry knew and remembered the very thing which in his letter he denies.

In this same examination of Mr. Dana it appeared that General Fry was expressly informed on the 2d of April, both by Mr. Dana and myself, that I was in Washington at the request of the Secretary of War, and that the subject of my visit was the alleged wrongs in recruiting in Haddock's division. The allegation under consideration, then, was certainly and intentionally false.

Let us look at the next step.

Second. "*Mr. Dana* had Mr. Conkling appointed to investigate all frauds in enlistment in western New York."

Did General Fry believe this statement when he wrote it? In a subsequent part of the letter he speaks of Mr. Dana as "his (my) friend Mr. Dana," and the imputation is that my employment was not the act of the Secretary of War, but was brought about by management and cuddling between Mr. Dana and myself.

If General Fry believed anything of this sort, he derived the impression somewhere and somehow. He saw something or heard something or other which led him to think so. What was it? Does any such crumb of evidence come to us on which charity can feed? He dare not testify that he had any reason to believe it, or that he did believe it. He did not believe it; had he done so even without evidence, but from sheer blind malignity, he would have spoken of it at some time to Mr. Stanton and been undeceived.

Let us go a little further:

Third. "With the stipulation that he should be *commissioned* judge advocate for the prosecution of any cases brought to trial, and he was *so appointed*," &c.

How came this statement to be made? It was not inadvertent, because upon it he founds a charge of very grave character. It is false, however. There is no evidence of its truth, but evidence of record to the contrary, which must have been familiar, and which is shown to have been familiar to General Fry. It looks like a studied statement for a carefully considered purpose, and it cannot have been innocently made.

But again:

Fourth. "*Mr. Dana vested him by several orders issued in the name of the Secretary of War, without the sanction of Mr. Stanton, with the most extraordinary powers.*"

Here are three printed lines, and four separate untruths.

1. It cannot be that General Fry believed that *Mr. Dana* did what was done at all. He was informed and knew to the contrary, as has been already shown.

2. "In the name of the Secretary of War." This is disproved by the papers themselves.

3. "Without the sanction of Mr. Stanton." We have the oath of Mr. Stanton and of Mr. Dana to the falsity of this. But let us suppose for a moment that it had been true, in order to test the integrity of General Fry. If it had been true, no one could have known it in the first place but Mr. Stanton and Mr. Dana, and any disclosure of it must have come from one of them. Indeed, the nature of General Fry's statement implies, and his language implies, that he speaks by authority of the Secretary of War. At all events, if General Fry made his statement in good faith, he must have supposed that Mr. Stanton or Mr. Dana had said something to warrant it. Both these gentlemen have been on the stand as witnesses, with full opportunity to General Fry and his counsel to cross-examine them. Did they venture to put any question going to show that it was pretended that either of them had ever hinted anything giving color to such an idea? It must not be forgotten here that all three of the papers referred to expressly state that they were made and given not only with the "sanction," but by the direct warrant, of the Secretary of War.

It must be remembered also that General Fry was pointedly informed, both before and after the papers were made, that the whole thing was the personal act of Secretary Stanton himself.

Yet in the face of all this, General Fry charges Mr. Dana with an official act not only surreptitious and dishonest, but amounting virtually to forgery.

Is this a malignant man? All unprincipled and untruthful men are not malignant. This inquiry is made of the committee at this point, because at another point it will be necessary to inquire whether General Fry is capable of waylaying the character or person of another; whether he is capable of suborning witnesses, or of seeking false evidence to stab the reputation of an enemy.

Look at the remaining statement in the three lines I am considering:

4. "With the most extraordinary powers." Mr. Dana and Mr. Stanton both prove that so far from this being true, the papers were ordinary *routine* papers, and conferred less than the powers commonly granted in similar cases familiar to General Fry.

Thus we see that the last quoted portion of the letter is knowingly false, not in some particular, but in every particular.

Please look at the next sentence and see whether it contains one single truth, or one innocent mistake. I quote : "Among these (the extraordinary powers) was the right to examine *the despatches in all telegraph offices* in the western division of New York, *which enabled a violation of the sanctity of personal and business correspondence."*

Here is a distinct assertion—*first*, that all despatches, or the despatches generally, in the various telegraph offices, were, by the terms of the authority, exposed to examination; and, *second*, that the sanctity of personal and business correspondence was in fact violated.

The first assertion is sufficiently refuted by the written authority itself. As will be seen, it is a request merely, and asks that access be afforded to such despatches as will lead to the detection of frauds, &c. Here it is in full :

WAR DEPARTMENT,
Washington City, April 3, 1865.

Honorable Roscoe Conkling having been appointed by the Secretary of War to investigate transactions connected with recruiting in the western division of New York, all telegraph companies and operators are respectfully requested to afford him access to any despatches which he may require for the purpose of detecting frauds and bringing criminals to trial.

By order of the Secretary of War :

C. A. DANA,
Assistant Secretary of War.

But the matter in this part of General Fry's statement which needs attention most, is the infamous suggestion that, under color of the authority given me, I looked into private and business correspondence.

Even if the authority were broad enough to admit of such abuse, what palliation is there for the assertion that it ever occurred ?

Does General Fry dare to present himself as a witness and testify that he ever heard or dreamed anything of the kind? On the contrary, he has been called upon repeatedly, in the presence of the committee, to come forward as a witness and purge himself. He has been notified, as the record shows, that it was charged and believed that he dare not submit himself to cross-examination; and yet he has refused, and has even submitted to the degradation of hearing his counsel announce, to go down on the record, that he declined to be cross-examined, and that if I obliged him to testify, or if the committee obliged him to testify, it must be as my own witness, and with the understanding that I should not be at liberty to impeach or contradict him !

I ask you, gentlemen, to contemplate the spectacle of a soldier and an officer publishing under his own signature charges of such a character, and then, when called upon to prove them or excuse them, being able to offer no legitimate evidence, and when required to testify to his own good faith in stating what he did, refusing to do so, and taking the ground, in so many words, that he will only testify upon compulsion, and then with the understanding that he shall not be impeached or contradicted !

Does not such a soldier stain the honor of his profession ? Should he administer a bureau, should he remain an officer of the American army, or should he "sleep in honor's truckle-bed ? "

Look, if you please, at the next sentence of this libel :

8

"For his services in this connexion Mr. Conkling received, on the 9th of November last, from the United States the *modest* fee of $3,000."

The essence of this statement is that the sum paid was excessive, and there is a suggestion running through the whole that the employment was improperly sought after, improperly obtained, and improperly charged for.

General Fry surely knew all these things to be untrue. Let us see if he did not.

He knew that the employment was not sought after. A letter has been put in evidence, written by me to General Fry, and brought here from his files, dated April 24, 1865, expressive of reluctance to go on with the service, and of a wish that I might be relieved. Mr. Stanton and Mr. Dana both testify that the employment was declined; that I named another lawyer and advised his selection, and consented to act only upon Mr. Stanton's urgent request. (See testimony of Mr. Stanton and Mr. Dana.) Besides, the record of Haddock's conviction, which General Fry is shown to have examined long ago, disclosed facts showing that the employment was not sought or obtained by any act of mine.

General Fry knew, also—for the same files of the department from which he learned that compensation had been made disclosed the fact—that the fee was not fixed by me, and that no charge whatever was ever made. He knew further that Mr. Stanton fixed the compensation, and he knew the general extent of the services, and the amount of money obtained by the government. This amount was not less than two hundred thousand dollars, besides the fine of ten thousand. (See the review of Judge Advocate General Holt, which is in evidence.)

Can it be supposed that General Fry believed that Mr. Stanton had fixed and paid an improper or excessive fee? If he knew the value of the services, or if he inquired of others who did know, he cannot have supposed the compensation was too much; and if he did not know and did not inquire, he cannot have believed that Mr. Stanton had acted in ignorance or bad faith.

As to the reasonableness of the allowance, General Fry has offered no evidence, but the committee has heard the testimony of several witnesses well qualified to speak. Judge Hunt says $5,000 would have been reasonable and just. This witness has a minute knowledge, as his examination proved, of all the particulars necessary to form a judgment of the value of the services, and his evidence shows, as does that of Mr. Roberts, an actual pecuniary loss sustained from the neglect and surrender of other professional business greater than the fee in question. Mr. Stanton swears to his opinion, and says that he thought at the time the allowance should have been $5,000 instead of $3,000.

Mr. Dana, who well knows what other persons received for professional services rendered the War Department, says $5,000 or $6,000 would have been moderate.

That we need not lack light on this subject, the committee called before it the head of the American bar, if any man is accorded that distinction. I was not present, but the record shows that in answer to the chairman of the committee, the Honorable Reverdy Johnson said $5,000 would have been a moderate charge for the service. And it was admitted by the counsel before the committee that such would be the testimony of other eminent lawyers.

The reasonableness of the fee paid is thoroughly established; the propriety, in fact, of its payment and receipt, cannot be questioned, and is not now questioned; and the committee will be able to say whether the *animus* of the pretence to the contrary could have been honest.

That the request to render the service was proper *in law*, that the rendition of the service was proper, and that it was right by law, technically, in form and substance, to make compensation on the one side and to receive it on the other, I shall endeavor to satisfy the committee in the proper place; but as that is a question of law, I will speak of it separately.

Let me first continue the examination of General Fry's statements of fact. He proceeds to say: " Whether he received, as has been reported, from his district $5,000 more for the same service, and whether he received additional fees from guilty parties for opposing proceedings at Utica, I am unable now to say."

The first statement here is under cover of an alleged rumor, and is in the form of insinuation. It would therefore have been competent for General Fry to prove anything verbal or written, by way of hearsay, or scandal even, that had reached him, and to which he had reference at the time he wrote his letter.

A member of the committee put to Mr. Roberts the question whether he had ever heard such a report. General Fry certainly knew, therefore, that that kind of evidence was available if he had it, yet no attempt has been made to prove that any human being ever whispered or hinted such a thing. If General Fry ever heard or heard of such a report, he was a competent witness, *the* witness of all others to state it, yet he recoils from the witness stand as he would from the sting of an adder.

The committee will see that such a report as is suggested never could have prevailed, for malice would never invent so preposterous and bungling a statement. Why? Because my district consists of one county—counties in New York are represented for such purposes only by boards of supervisors—and the statutes of the State require accounts of moneys to be so kept and so published that no sum could have been paid for such an object by any custodian of public money without the records showing it to the world. The proposition is upon its face impossible and absurd.

The second branch of this atrocious accusation is not pretended to be founded on rumor—it is stated as a belief generated in the mind of the writer by something he knows. He then states, in substance, that he can mention something tending to account for his belief, and straightway he proceeds to yet another deliberate untruth, which, as we shall see in a moment, was intentional.

But, first of all, what will the committee say of a man capable of making such a charge without an atom of evidence to substantiate it, or to explain his making it?

The next words in this letter are these: " But, as hereafter shown, he was as zealous in preventing prosecutions at Utica as he was in making them at Elmira; and the main ground of difficulty between Mr. Conkling and myself has been that I wanted exposure at both places, while he wanted concealment at one. I suppose there can be no doubt among high-minded men as to the character of Mr. Conkling's course in this matter." An effort has been made to change this assertion from a bald and naked falsehood, into a reference to something that General Fry believed had occurred in relation to the following persons: Captain J. P. Richardson, provost marshal, dismissed December, 1864; Captain P. B. Crandall, provost marshal, suspended March 13, 1865; discharged May 31, 1865, Aaron Richardson, of Albany, the accomplice of Haddock.

The attempted explanation only aggravates the crime of making the charge, because the explanation is in bad faith in each instance. Let us see.

The effort to conjure up anything of the kind in the case of J. P. Richardson was a fraud upon the committee, and a wretched subterfuge. There could be no possible room for General Fry to suppose that I wanted concealment as to Captain Richardson, or that I had prevented any prosecution against him. He knew to the contrary. In the first place, the only part I took as to the removal of Captain Richardson was to advise and ask for publicity and investigation, that we might know what, if any, wrongs had been done. My action was all in connexion with that of numerous leading citizens, and no malice could honestly torture it into impropriety.

This appears from letters brought from the files of the War Department, from the following citizens of Utica: Hon. William J. Bacon, Hon. Ward Hunt,

Ellis H. Roberts, esq., T. R. Walker, esq., Erastus Clark, esq., Charles H. Hopkins, esq., and others. These men are neither "drunkards," "cowards," "thieves," nor "sneaks," nor are they " demoralized" or "dishonest," as Mr. Dana testifies General Fry said all the people in Oneida county were, and their letters as to Captain Richardson, concurred in by me, demanding investigation, tell too plain a tale to leave any escape from the conclusion that the pretence is dishonest that General Fry supposed concealment was sought in the case of Captain Richardson.

But, again, in December, 1864, more than three months before I was requested to prosecute Haddock, or to make any investigation for the government, General Fry wrote to me (see the letter) that the charges against Captain Richardson had been placed in the hands of William A. Dart, United States district attorney, at Pottsdam, New York, upwards of two hundred miles from my residence. He knew, therefore, that in April, 1865, Captain Richardson was not and had not for months been connected with the Provost Marshal's bureau, or with the military service, and that his case had been specially handed over to the civil tribunals, and placed in the hands of the regular prosecuting officer there. Yet, in the face of all this, General Fry has the hardihood to pretend that he meant in his letter merely to say that I ought to have prosecuted Captain Richardson, and omitted to do it. This is a mere fetch; it is in the face of all light and knowledge. General Fry knew that I advised that Captain Richardson's acts should be investigated at once upon his removal; he knew that I never, by word or act, put any obstacle in the way; he knew that I was never instructed or authorized to take charge of the case, but that it was specially placed in other hands, and therefore he knew that I could not have neglected the matter, much less been " zealous in preventing prosecution."

The attempt to escape from the responsibility of this groundless charge, by pretending that it refers to an omission to prosecute Captain Crandall, is, if possible, more unpardonable and false than the same pretence in the case of Captain Richardson.

The proof is conclusive that there was no room for criticism in this regard in connexion with Captain Crandall. Immediately upon the suspension of this officer I forwarded to General Fry all the information I had relating to the matter, although under no obligation beyond any other citizen to do so.

A letter on the subject received from Mr. Secretary Dana was handed to Mr. Hunt, with the request that he would answer it, which he did in full, Mr. Roberts and other citizens at the same time communicating fully to General Fry by telegraph and letter, all the light they could give.

In transmitting the evidence within my knowledge, I expressed to General Fry, the opinion that Captain Crandall was honest, and that the wrong was with Haddock, and the proofs at the same time enclosed to him fully sustained this belief. (See the letters, etc., enclosed to General Fry, March 13.)

On the 2d and 3d of April General Fry had before him all the charges which he and Haddock had been able to invent or collect against Captain Crandall, and they covered all the aspersions which have ever been put upon him.

In addition to this, he had caused an inspection to be made of Captain Crandall's doings, by an officer selected by himself, who went under " verbal instructions" from General Fry, the spirit of which may be inferred from what has appeared in the case, and the result of this "inspection" was before him, as were also full reports from Captain Crandall and his counsel as to the $20,000 of bonds.

In the light of all this, General Fry, on the 2d of April, (Sunday,) admitted twice over to Mr. Dana and to me that he knew of nothing upon the case as stated which Captain Crandall should have done or omitted which he had not done or omitted! (See Mr. Dana's evidence.)

Add to this that, in the presence of the committee at the War Department,

General Fry admitted, in answer to a question from the Secretary of War, that he never had charged Captain Crandall with wrong, and never had supposed he could be prosecuted, and we shall have some idea of the good faith of pretending now that Captain Crandall should have been tried. Knowing as General Fry did, and as he knew the Secretary did, that I believed entirely in Captain Crandall's integrity, morally, as Luddington did "legally," he, of course, cannot have supposed that I was to prosecute Crandall. No imbecility on his part would admit of such a supposition, and hence there is no room for believing that an omission to prosecute Crandall can have appeared to General Fry a violation of the duty assigned by the "appointment," as he calls it, of April 3.

Again : General Fry knew that no proposal had ever been made by him or any one else to have charges drawn against Captain Crandall, or a court-martial ordered to try him, and without this, as he well knew, Captain Crandall could not be tried.

He knew also that, on the 31st of May, he himself "discharged" Captain Crandall from the service; that he did not *dismiss* him, nor dishonorably discharge him, nor hold him for trial, nor keep him relieved till further investigation, but that he discharged him. (See order.)

He knew also that in the Haddock trial the alleged wrongs at the Utica office were fully investigated ; that Crandall was shown to be the foe throughout of the operations of Aaron Richardson and other brokers with whom Haddock was colluding, and that the idea of prosecuting Crandall would have provoked only indignation and derision wherever the facts were known.

He knew also that I had no part in selecting Captain Crandall as provost marshal ; that I merely concurred in the selection made by others who deemed Captain Crandall eminently trustworthy; and that, in expressing confidence in his integrity, after Haddock marked him for destruction, I only united with the most honored citizens of the district, and only uttered the voice of the whole community. Nevertheless, and in the face of the positive evidence of Judge Hunt and Mr. Roberts that I declined to take part in selecting a provost marshal, and that Captain Crandall was selected wholly by others, I only forwarding the name and concurring in it, the counsel of General Fry here to-day indulge the malevolence of their client by insisting that Captain Crandall was selected by me " exclusively," as they put it.

He knew also that the facts and results fully vindicated the confidence expressed in Crandall.

But let us pass on.

The attempt of General Fry to maintain the imputation of suppressing prosecutions while pretending to conduct them, by giving evidence in relation to the arrest of Aaron Richardson, and his release without trial, is more infamous than almost any other proceeding witnessed by the committee.

Patrick J. Kinney did not appear on either list of witnesses asked for by General Fry ; his name was never handed to the committee, nor to any member of it, nor was a summons applied for, until after he had been brought to Washington. He was brought to Washington surreptitiously. He was telegraphed by General Fry, May 23, to come to his "office," and again May 24. He did come, and saw General Fry in person, and informed him of what he knew ; and after this, General Fry introduced him as a witness, with the deliberate design of creating an inference which he knew to be as false as it was blasting. The undeniable intention of General Fry was to create the impression or suspicion that I had been guilty of a wrong, and had acted in collusion with Richardson, or for his benefit, and not in the interest of the government, when I gave the officers about to carry him away under arrest to understand that he was making disclosures to the government.

Consider such an act ! General Fry all the while knew that Aaron Richardson was the accomplice through whom largely came out the evidence of Haddock's guilt. This fact was notorious, and was proved by the record of Haddock's conviction.

The record also showed fully the arrest of Richardson, and my entire connexion with it, and General Fry's letter shows that he examined this record at an early day.

If he did not know that the Secretary of War and the Judge Advocate General had directed that Aaron Richardson should be used as a witness, or if he ever honestly suspected there was anything wrong about Aaron Richardson's not being tried, he most certainly would have asked the Secretary, or at least have referred to the record at once.

In any aspect, this act of General Fry is without any excuse. If the charge in his letter had reference to Aaron Richardson, it was groundless and malicious; and whether his letter referred to this man, or whether he trumped up, afterward, the allegation that it did, the covert effort which has been witnessed to create an impression known to be false, and of so injurious a character, evinces a turpitude almost incredible.

Look at the next passage of this letter:

"As to the *animus* of Mr. Conkling's calumnious assault upon me, it is true (notwithstanding his assertion that he had no personal quarrels with me) that the differences between him and myself arose altogether from my unwillingness to gratify him in certain matters in which he had a strong personal interest. It is true also that he was foiled in his efforts to obtain undue concessions from my bureau, and to discredit me in the eyes of my superiors."

Is any part of this true? No proof is offered sustaining any part of it, but its falsity is affirmatively established.

Mr. Dana testifies that there never was any matter in which I had any interest whatever at the War Department or at any bureau in it. If there was any such matter it was easy to point it out.

Even upon his own showing General Fry has here misrepresented the most trifling incident in this statement, viz: that I was foiled in efforts to discredit him in the eyes of his superiors. The only instance he attempts to give of any such effort, is the letter to Mr. Dana, containing charges against Haddock, and saying that General Fry, if pure himself, is imposed upon. If this was an effort to "discredit" him, I certainly was not "foiled" in it, inasmuch as the Secretary of War put Haddock upon trial and selected me to prosecute him. If I had been "foiled" in having Haddock brought to justice, I might have escaped, and my district might have escaped, the vengeance of an unprincipled official.

Let me go to the next assertion in this letter:

"There have been three main issues between Mr. Conkling and myself. The first arose in consequence of the removal of Captain Richardson, (the first provost marshal of Mr. Conkling's district,) upon a report of Judge Advocate Turner that the proofs in his case disclosed a reckless persistence in fraudulent practices. Mr. Conkling complained of my action both to the President and War Department, but failed to procure any modification of my course."

This statement, as the correspondence which alone could sustain it shows, is utterly groundless.

There was no "complaint" whatever. The letter to the President was signed by many citizens as well as myself—among them, Judge Bacon, Mr. Walker, Mr. Clark and Mr. Roberts—and the representations it contained related to Major Haddock and not to General Fry.

He next says: "The second issue was as to the restoring of Captain Crandall, (the second provost marshal of the district,) after I had secured his removal from duty on the recommendation of Major Ludington, who thoroughly inspected the district, and reported that though not legally guilty he had morally perpetrated a most glaring and inexcusable fraud on the government he was sworn to serve, and that he had quieted his conscience by casuistry and regulated his actions by the counsel of unscrupulous legal advisers. Mr. Conkling failed to get Captain Crandall restored, and the officer selected by me continued in charge of the business until the office was closed."

This curiously illustrates General Fry's want of singleness of purpose even in misstatement.

Captain Crandall was suspended and removed from duty March 13, two weeks before Major Ludington recommended anything. He was never suspended further, till May 31, when he was finally discharged. In one of his printed letters in the Globe General Fry states that Crandall was "suspended from office" on the 9th of March because he did not turn over the bonds.

But the important fact here is, that Luddington's report was dated March 31, and my sole act after that, as to Captain Crandall, was a simple recommendation or expression of opinion. And yet General Fry makes the statement I have read.

What next? "The *third issue was as to the government's employing counsel to defend Captain Crandall after he* had been relieved, and *had carried with him*, in violation of the orders of the *department*, some twenty thousand dollars *local bounty* deposited with him *in behalf of recruits*, and in regard to which he got into litigation.

"In *this Mr. Conkling failed*. Counsel has not, to my knowledge, been authorized, nor have any lawyers been paid by the government in that suit."

In general, this passage is intended to convey the idea that I was seeking some advantage to myself or to others from the government. It is groundless and malicious taken together, and its particulars are all wilfully distorted in order to deepen the injury to be done.

1. There never was any *issue* whatever on the subject. I did nothing in regard to it except to forward a letter to the War Department with the recommendation that attention should be given to the matter.

2. I never proposed or suggested the employment of counsel, or any other action, for the purpose alleged, to wit, "defending Crandall." On the contrary, as proved by Judge Hunt, Crandall had no interest in the matter, one way or the other. He never claimed, and could not claim, a farthing either way.

The whole question was, whether the government should assert its right to $20,000 of bonds; and I had no part nor lot in the matter save to transmit, when requested to do so, a statement of facts to the government.

3. It is equally false that Captain Crandall " carried with him " these bonds, and, if possible, still more false that he had done so "in violation of the orders of the department." He never carried the bonds anywhere, but, on the contrary, he sacredly deposited them in a bank, and at once advised the " department " that he had done so.

When Major Haddock sought to possess himself of them for uses of plunder, as was believed, Captain Crandall consulted eminent counsel as to his duty, and was advised to preserve the bonds until the facts could be represented to General Fry, and his direction obtained. Elaborate and respectful statements, in duplicate, were at once forwarded to General Fry, through Major Haddock, and also directly. The facts were given minutely, and his direction solicited. This was repeated again and again. He was specially asked to direct Crandall to turn over the bonds to the government. But all to no purpose. He maintained a contemptuous silence, broken only by puerile and incoherent inquiries, showing an incapacity, almost imbecile, or else a poorly disguised privity with plunderers.

4. These bonds were not "local bounty," nor were they " deposited in behalf of recruits." On the contrary, as was repeatedly explained to General Fry at the time, in a way so simple and clear as to come within his comprehension, they were pledged, not as bounty at all, not in behalf of recruits, but as security against desertion, and by a recruit *broker*.

An effort was made to induce the government to claim and hold the bonds that the amount might go to the treasury. General Fry, by stupidity or dishonest neglect, trifled them away, utterly and persistently withholding aid or direction, until at length the county of Oneida volunteered to contest the case with the broker.

For directing the attention of the War Department to the propriety of looking after this sum of money, and securing it to the public treasury, an act for which there could have been no possible motive, selfish or personal, I am subjected by an unprincipled delinquent to a scurrilous imputation.

The assertions as to Captain Crandall and the bonds conclude with a fling about my efforts to invoke the attention of the government having "failed." It will be some one's duty, in the future stages of this investigation, when that range of evidence is in order, to show *why* those efforts "failed," and the same evidence may show also, perhaps, why we have "failed" in all efforts to conx or drive General Fry to the witness stand, where he could be cross-examined and exposed.

Here is General Fry's next statement:

" In support of his denial of differences with me which influenced his action Mr. Conkling states the fact that we had but one personal interview. That is true, but it proves the reverse of what Mr. Conkling asserts, for it was of such a nature as to render other interviews very objectionable. I was called to Mr. Dana's office to have a verbal discussion with Mr. Conkling on the questions at issue, but I had by this time learned too much of this gentleman to transact business with him in that way, and I declined to do so. We had, directly and indirectly, much correspondence, and generally of an unpleasant character, and I presume under such circumstances it will be granted that men's personal relations will be bad, although they may have had but one personal interview."

I propose at this point to consider this statement as to its own truth or falsehood merely. It is one of several passages in the letter designed among other things to disprove my denial in the House of having had personal "quarrels" with General Fry, in which "quarrels" I was "worsted."

When I come to the last of these passages I will consider them together, and show the groundlessness of the charge they are inserted to sustain. But, first, let me show how essentially devoid of truth they are separately, and now how untrue this one is.

Mr. Dana, while fixing the brand of falsehood upon General Fry in many other instances, does not omit this. He testifies as to this interview very minutely and positively; and how shall we escape the conclusion that General Fry, in pretending to give an account of it, was guilty of the most degrading misrepresentation?

Mr. Dana testifies that General Fry was not called in, as he says he was, "to have a verbal discussion with Mr. Conkling," but to explain something in the papers concerning Haddock, which was not intelligible from the papers themselves.

This is comparatively a small discrepancy at first view; it might almost be deemed accidental if it stood alone, but the rest of the sentence shows it to be a studied untruth, written in malice.

The letter says: "I had by this time learned too much of this gentleman to transact business with him in that way, and I declined to do so."

Mr. Dana testifies that General Fry was informed, on entering the room, that the Secretary of War had summoned Mr. Conkling to Washington in regard to Major Haddock, and the witness then narrates what followed.

Did General Fry "decline to discuss" the matter? On the contrary, he proceeded to indorse and eulogize Haddock, and to stigmatize as corrupt those who accused him or questioned his character or conduct. He said those who suspected Haddock were themselves dishonest. He declared that he had asked an investigation for Haddock in order to enable Haddock to vindicate himself, a result which doubtless would have been reached had the proceeding been, as was intended, under the auspices of General Fry.

After admitting himself unable to say that Captain Crandall had done wrong, he proceeded to asperse the whole people of Oneida county as "*demoralized and dishonest*," and denounced them as "*drunkards, thieves, and cowards*." (See Mr. Dana's testimony.)

Mr. Dana says General Fry did most of the talking, nobody disputing with him, quarrelling with him, or in any way impeding him in the exhibition he made. Having fully expressed himself in this choice language of a soldier and an official, he was allowed to retire.

This is the interview of which he has dared to publish the version already referred to; and in continuance of his assertion that he was "quarrelled" with, he adds, that "much correspondence" has occurred between himself and me, "generally of an unpleasant character."

Where is this correspondence? General Fry's habit of treasuring letters from all quarters, whether private or not, and his freedom in making use of them, renders it certain that had any such correspondence occurred, it would have been produced, or at least sworn to by some one.

General Fry next parades in various forms the assertion that he did not sustain Haddock "a day" after he had "proper evidence" of his being unworthy, and then adds that he required "better testimony than Hon. Roscoe Conkling." He says, further, that he approved of Haddock being tried; that he suspended him from duty, and wanted him punished, not for the crimes with which Mr. Conkling charged him, but for those of which he "was really guilty," and he asserts that Major Haddock pointed out to him "instances of unfairness in his trial." This part of the letter is within the present branch of the investigation, because it assails the truth of statements made on the floor by me. The attention of the committee is invited to these statements and insinuations separately.

1. Is it true that General Fry did not sustain Haddock after he had evidence of his unworthiness; or is it true that he upheld him after knowledge was brought home to him again and again of the most crying abuses, and until at last they became so flagrant that the Secretary of War suddenly took the matter in hand and arrested Haddock in mid career?

It will be remembered that Luddington's report was dated March 31, 1865, and General Fry professes to have presented it to the Secretary of War April 1. Two days at least before this Mr. Stanton, as he himself testifies, had telegraphed me to come to Washington for the purpose of having Haddock tried. Colonel Tracy testifies that he arrested Haddock on the order of the Secretary of War, which reached him April 4, and that Haddock was then in full blast in his office at Elmira.

It cannot be denied that General Fry sustained Haddock most zealously up to April 1, which was some days after Mr. Stanton had determined to put him on trial, and yet the evidence shows conclusively that during a whole month General Fry had before him such information of the corrupt practices of his favorite as no honest man could ignore. Indeed, the proof already admitted as falling within even the narrow limits of the present branch of the investigation points to instances of guilt in Haddock, so far abetted by General Fry as to more than suggest a criminal collusion between them.

On the 28th of February, 1865, Peter A. La France transmitted to General Fry a lengthy written statement setting forth with much particularity various guilty practices in Major Haddock, of which he offered proof.

It is difficult to read this catalogue of accusations and see how a man of such capacity for believing as General Fry lays claim to, can have dismissed it uncared for. It is still more difficult to understand how he could have referred it to Haddock himself, as he informed the committee he "presumes he did."

Haddock was afterwards convicted of the offences charged by La France, but General Fry did not deem the matter worth his while. "One swallow proves not spring," and one contradiction of an assertion of General Fry ought not, perhaps, to impeach it; let us see if his assertion last referred to is further contradicted.

Edward Maloy, a detective of the War Department, was sent in February to Utica to make a secret inspection. He did so, and reported that nothing was wrong with the officers there. He was then sent by Baker to Elmira. There he made a thorough inspection, and detected Haddock in the same kind of official corruption which La France alleged. This was February 25. He found two bounty brokers, Dalton and Weibel, in collusion with Haddock, and made his report at once to Baker, accusing all three. Baker came to Washington, and laid the matter before General Fry. Forthwith Dalton and Weibel were arrested, tried, convicted, and sent to the penitentiary.

Maloy's report, to borrow General Fry's language, was "*proper evidence*" for the incarceration of two of three confederates in crime; but Haddock being the third, justice was satisfied without molesting him; it was enough to exterminate the vermin, without expecting to disgrace a favorite of a sagacious superior, so Haddock rolled on.

If any part of Maloy's statement is untrue, Colonel Baker knows it, General Fry knows it; where are they?

Let us go a little further:

March 11 and 12, Judge Hunt, Mr. Roberts, Mr. Hopkins, Mr. Walker, and others, telegraphed and wrote to General Fry, directly and positively charging Haddock with the most flagrant corruption.

Was this "proper evidence," at least to put General Fry upon inquiry? Was it proper evidence for him to communicate to the Secretary of War or to some one?

Is it pretended that any use was made of it?

March 12 or 13, Captain Crandall and Commissioner Munroe having furnished me with many facts from which the guilt of Haddock was palpable, and these facts having been put upon paper, together with verbatim copies of letters and despatches implicating Haddock, the whole was put in print for General Fry's convenience, and transmitted to him. The committee is asked to examine these printed statements, and see whether for disregarding them at the time, and for asserting now that they afforded no "proper evidence" for action, General Fry can be acquitted of corruption except by being convicted of incapacity beyond belief.

No act or omission in this connexion stamps General Fry with delinquency more than the report of Luddington, and the orders which led to it.

Luddington was an officer selected by General Fry. What for? What does he say, in his application to the Secretary of War, he wants Luddington placed at his disposal for? To make inspection at *New York, Elmira, and Utica*. He obtained, upon this application, an order directing Luddington to report to him (General Fry) for "verbal instructions." Now, look at the report and see what instructions General Fry gave him. With all the proofs of Haddock's venality heaped up before him, did he direct Luddington to inspect at Elmira? With all the nauseating details of the corrupt burlesque at New York and Hoboken, of which I will speak presently, before him, did he direct Luddington to inspect at New York? Oh, no. "The board of enrolment of the 21st district of New York"—that was the sole object to which General Fry instructed Luddington to direct his inspection. Why? The board was already suspended, and the administration there in the hands of those selected by General Fry and Haddock themselves. Everything was safe. What was the need of an inspection there post haste?

What sort of instructions does the committee suppose General Fry gave this officer thus despatched? What is the value and what the mockery of such an *ex parte* investigation thus inspired by General Fry? But Luddington went, and returned with a long report, saying that he had been instructed to inspect the 21st district, and then detailing all that he heard against that district, and at the end it just barely crops out that "*incident* to the inspection of the 21st district"—mark the expression, "incident" to this—"facts were educed which led me to the conviction that Major John A. Haddock is unfit for the position he holds."

This innocent inspector having let the cat out of the bag, by showing in his report that he was to do nothing, and did nothing, but to inspect the Utica district, with still more guileless simplicity discloses that, as he understood what was expected of him, the enormities of Haddock, who ruled over fourteen congressional districts, were "incidental," and of no account; but when he stumbled over some of them two hundred miles from Elmira, where Haddock's headquarters were, he just makes a charcoal dot by the wayside.

In this place let it be remembered that though, on the 3d of April, General Fry was expressly directed by the Secretary of War to deliver to me all the papers bearing upon Haddock's case, I was compelled to prepare the charges and specifications without them, and on the 24th of April was still writing for them. The charges were filed April 14. (See letter.)

Does any member of this committee doubt, if we pause at this point, that Haddock was improperly screened by General Fry? He casts an imputation upon me by denying that he had evidence against Haddock, save that which came from me, and by alleging that evidence from me was unworthy of confidence; but the proof fixes upon him malicious falsehood, if it does not establish collusion with Haddock beside.

Let us pass to the second portion of this same passage in which General Fry attests his willingness to have Haddock tried, and his action to that end.

It is not true that he suspended Haddock from duty, as we have seen.

It is not true that he approved of Haddock's being tried.

Mr. Dana shows that he declared, after doing what he calls suspending him from duty, that he had done so in order that such an investigation might be had *as would vindicate Haddock.*

Mr. Dana shows, also, how excited and agitated he was at learning that I was to try Haddock.

Mr. Dana says he acted like a man greatly disturbed "internally," and "constrained." What about? Why, if there was nothing between himself and Haddock, should he be confounded at the tidings that a lawyer had been sent for to prosecute Haddock, whether guilty or innocent?

"What's he to Hecuba, or Hecuba to him?"

What is meant by wanting Haddock punished for the crimes of which he was really guilty, "not for those with which Mr. Conkling charged him?"

The court before which he was tried convicted him of every charge made against him. He was convicted also of every aggravated specification, either literally or substantially, and these charges and specifications contain every accusation I ever made against him.

General Fry knows this, and he also knows that the Judge Advocate General, in reviewing the case finally, says that there was a superabundance of evidence to uphold the findings; that the turpitude of the accused was almost without example, and that the sentence was surprisingly light. (See the review by Judge Holt.)

This false fling in Haddock's behalf is only the outgrowth of the affinity between them.

Of the same character is the aspersion cast upon the court and upon the Sec-

2

retary of War, and the President, who approved and executed the sentence, by the assertion that there were "instances of unfairness" in the trial.

I wish now to gather up and ask attention to all parts of this letter which challenge my veracity. A man who stands convicted over and over again, by the oaths of his official superiors and of others, as well as by records, of the most despicable and malicious falsifying, and who has meanly impugned the characters of many persons, may not have expected much stress to be laid upon a mere charge of untruthfulness. But I ask the committee to scrutinize this issue thoroughly.

The point is upon my having had "quarrels" with General Fry, in which "quarrels" I was "worsted." Because I denied that assertion General Fry has charged me with falsehood.

The letter opens by affirming the truth of the assertion which I had denied, and then follow several statements introduced to show its truth. Each one of these statements has been proved conclusively to be false.

But, without confining the inquiry to the matter referred to by General Fry, where can a shadow of defence be found for this reiterated statement?

1. If the attempt of General Fry to screen Haddock, and my effort to uncover him, could be deemed a "quarrel," certainly I was not worsted in it. But of course it was in no sense a quarrel, either with Haddock or General Fry, any more than any prosecuting counsel is to be deemed to quarrel with the felon whom he tries, or with his accomplices or sympathizers.

I ask the committee to consider the repeated instances in this letter in which General Fry directly and indirectly imputes to me a want of veracity because I repelled the assertion that I had had "quarrels" with him, in which I was "worsted;" and a report is earnestly asked for upon the question whether the denial I made subjected my veracity to any just aspersion.

I have now gone through this letter as far as it reflects upon me—and that is as far as you have allowed me to go—and I have shown it to be a tissue of base and groundless calumnies. Aspersing, as it does, several persons besides myself, it was written and published in bad faith, and for the purpose of blackening public and private character. The act was in defiance of the privileges of the House of Representatives, in violation of the rules and articles of war, and of the official oath of the writer, and a breach of the regulations of the department in which General Fry is a subordinate. To this is to be added the failure before the committee to give any excuse, the refusal to testify himself, and the effort to manufacture a defence by sinister and disingenuous offers of testimony, and statements of what witnesses were expected to prove. Here, in one aspect, I might stop, because the duty of the committee and of the House is already rendered clear. The turpitude involved, the flagrant character of the offences, and the infraction they constitute of the military law to which General Fry is amenable, first as a soldier, second as an officer, and again as an executive officer of the government, would before any tribunal point to but one result. Malicious falsehood, denominated in the military code "lying," alone, as the committee is aware, is one of the most heinous crimes an officer can commit. Mere cowardice is punished with the last severity and ignominy; but what cowardice could be more detestable than that which, having sought by false accusations to destroy character, skulks away both from reparation and responsibility, and, having no other proof to substantiate its assertions, shrinks from the ordeal of a personal examination, and, even upon an investigation like this, resorts to the attempt to fabricate and sustain fresh imputations known to be false? If the evidence has this extent, it would seem to be painfully abundant.

But the worst yet remains to be told. General Fry stands convicted, beyond all this, of official delinquency, with which the committee must deal.

In the branch of the investigation which is about to close, the committee has observed a rule of evidence which has, for the time being, shielded General

Fry from all proof of general misconduct, such as will come within the range of the branch of the investigation reserved for the future. No evidence has been admissible against General Fry thus far, unless it bore distinctly upon one of two points. It must show the falsity of some statement in the letter relating to me, or else it must show to the motive with which the letter was written and published.

Restricted to this narrow range, the evidence reveals a state of facts and fixes them past controversy, in the face of which no man, by the laws of this country, can remain the head of a bureau or an officer of the army.

General Fry has had the fullest opportunity to answer the proof referred to in any and every way. Every mode known to me has been resorted to to induce him to make denial by his own oath, but in vain. He steadily, by the advice of counsel, one of them a military officer, as well as a lawyer, has declined to present himself as a witness. He has even omitted, after deliberation, to call other witnesses who could certainly contradict the testimony to which I refer, if, indeed, it had been false. Instead of this, he has offered letters and despatches, written by himself, and papers of other kinds, which, it will be found, are not to the purpose.

If after this full opportunity, in his own defence, General Fry is found to be guilty of the gravest official and personal crimes, it is believed that the committee, under its responsibilities, must so pronounce, and must recommend such action also as is called for by the facts. I will endeavor to put before you, as briefly as I may, the results of the evidence now referred to.

In the first place let me bring together the facts which must be treated as incontestable.

In February, 1865, a scheme was set on foot, General Fry being privy to it, to "capture bounty jumpers and deserters" at Hoboken, New Jersey, a locality historic for tragic occurrences and startling effects. The plan in brief was this: A recruiting office was to be opened, and "bounty jumpers" were to be baited and enticed until it should become a crowded resort, and then, when the time was ripe, great numbers were to be "bagged," in the phrase which seems to have been employed.

The *modus operandi* was to be as follows: Day by day a limited number of "jumpers" were to be enlisted, and to be paid the amount of local bounty being paid at the time in New Jersey to volunteers, and then they were to be immediately allowed and induced to desert, carrying their bounty with them. These "jumpers" were expected to spread the news of the Hoboken "walk away" to the other "jumpers" around about, and as the fame of it went abroad, more and more "jumpers" were looked for to come, and at the appointed day all who came were to be taken in and held under arrest. The operation began on or about the 4th of March, and from four to seven "jumpers" a day were enlisted, paid six hundred dollars each or thereabout, and taken to the back door, and suffered to depart. On the 10th of March, 183 "jumpers" were enlisted, and in place of being passed out the back door, were passed up a stairs into a room, where they were held. They were transferred thence to Fort Lafayette, and there confined a month or so, and then discharged without trial.

This is the naked statement of the first chapter of this history, putting it in the light most favorable to General Fry, and, before going to the worse stages of it, I wish to direct attention to one or two considerations. The plot was very unique. Men were enlisted as soldiers, and paid large bounties on purpose to have them desert, which they were allowed and induced to do confessedly with the connivance of General Fry. Of course it was not expected to punish these men for thus deserting, because the government was itself made the instigator. But it is explained to us that the purpose was through those who thus deserted by collusion to allure others to come that they might be arrested. Arrested for what? For some past desertion or other crime? How could this be? If there were men who could be identified, and held, and convicted for any offence previously committed, how could it be necessary, how could it be even an honest farce, to go through the ceremony of enlisting them as soldiers, merely as a mode of arrest, merely as a mode of taking their persons into custody?

It cannot be said, either, that, having been mustered into the military service, any of them were to be held for the act of being thus mustered in, without deserting afterwards.

What, then, is the apology for the Provost Marshal General of the United States being a party to such a transaction, even if this were the whole of it? But let us see what further is undisputed.

These "jumpers," thus to be enlisted without any design that they should ever enter the military service, but with a positive design that they should not, *were to be credited upon quotas and returned and counted as so many recruits furnished to the army.*

This was by a private order issued by General Fry himself, and produced to the committee.

It will be observed that this order was not issued as orders usually are, through a subordinate, but by *General Fry in person*, and marked "*special and confidential.*" (See the order.)

It is not denied—it cannot be denied—that this order had reference to these fraudulent and fictitious enlistments, and that it was issued expressly to cover them, and for no other purpose.

If there is anything to palliate this; if General Fry had any understanding of facts, or considerations which excused it; if he was a dupe in the matter, he knows it, and he could state it. Truth is never left to stand alone. If there was an honest or an innocent reason for this, however mistaken it may have been, or however hard it may be to imagine it, General Fry would have been safe in stating it; nay, would he not have been impelled to state it?

But let us go a little further. Not only were these men to be "credited" as soldiers, *but a firm of bounty brokers were, by an understanding with General Fry, to be allowed to sell these "credits," to any locality which would pay the highest price for them.*

Perhaps I am not literally correct in speaking of this as an uncontested fact. Let us see whether it is controverted or even denied.

It is admitted that local bounties were to be advanced to the men at the time of enlistment; at all events, this was to be so up to the last day. This was, of course, an indispensable part of the scheme. It is admitted, also, that Allen, Hughes & Riley were to furnish these bounties, as they did do in fact. It is not even suggested that these brokers were put in funds to pay the bounties, but it is conceded that they provided the money themselves. It follows that the only way they could reimburse themselves for these advances, indeed the only way they could keep themselves in funds to pay the bounties day by day, amounting as they did to several thousand dollars daily, was to dispose of the credits and realize upon them at once. It cannot be denied that the recruiting officer who acted under the orders of General Fry, the provost marshal of the district to which the credits were sold, the authorities of that district, the brokers themselves, and all concerned in the transaction, whether privy to it, or imposed upon by it, acted upon the idea that the credits were to be sold as they were in fact sold, and there is nothing to show that there was any different design on the part of General Fry, but, on the contrary, everything shows that he intended and arranged that the sale should take place.

It must not be forgotten either, that Allen swears that his firm paid the entire expenses of all kinds of the Hoboken exploit, and this fact is nowhere denied or disproved.

Having thus spoken of what it was intended to do, let us come to what was done.

Having sold credits for all of these enlistments made previous to March 10, having received the money, and having in several ways General Fry's indorsement of the act, Allen & Co. and Lieutenant Colonel Ilges (the officer detailed by General Fry to do the business pursuant to an arrangement between General Fry and Allen) proceeded on the 10th of March, as has been stated, to muster in one hundred and eighty-three "bounty jumpers." The same proceedings in all respects were taken as to these that had been taken as to their predecessors, except that they were not induced or allowed to desert, and no bounty was paid to them or to most of them. But they were regularly examined, enlisted, and mustered in, their enlistment papers and muster-rolls made out and certified and signed by Colonel Ilges, who, it is fair to say, seems to have acted under protest at every step. All this being done, *these credits were sold to Jersey City by Allen & Co. with the knowledge of Colonel Ilges, and General Fry was at once informed of it. The papers were handed over to the mayor of Jersey City, and he paid Allen & Co. for the credits the sum of one hundred and twenty-five or one hundred and twenty-six thousand dollars.*

At the time the money was paid Colonel Ilges referred to a general order which he said he should enforce in the case before him, and which required the mustering officer to detain from the broker $300 per man for every man put in by him. This amounted to $54,000, which Ricley, the member of the firm of Allen & Co., who seems to have acted as cashier, thereupon paid to Colonel Ilges under the requirement already stated.

It may be useful to bear in mind what sort of a fund this $54,000 was, and where, in fair dealing in cases of ordinary enlistments, it would have belonged. Had the enlistments been *bona fide*, and had the men gone to the field, the $300 per man would have belonged to the recruits; had they deserted, the $300 per man would at once have become deserters' money, and been turned over as such to the United States.

These men did not go into service, but were treated as deserters, though presently discharged, and it would seem that if, imposed upon by the appearances held out by those who for this purpose represented the government, Jersey City was led to pay its money in good faith for the credits, and the money, or any part of it, afterwards came under the control of the government, the natural and just course was this: the credits should have been allowed, on the ground that they had been honestly paid for under circumstances for which they were responsible, whose acts bound the government as to innocent third persons, and the money should have gone into the treasury. It is submitted that, unless some agreement made by General Fry, or some act of his, changed the original rights of the parties, this was the situation of the matter at the time of which I am about to speak.

Mr. Stanton took the same view, in part at least, as appears from his order made afterwards, which shows that he felt constrained, even by what came to his knowledge, to hold that Jersey City had so far acted upon the faith of acts done in the name of the government, that the credits given could not justly be revoked.

Let us see now what became of this $54,000—what General Fry did in regard to it, and how his conduct reflects upon this case.

This brings us to the testimony of Theodore Allen, and the testimony which corroborates Theodore Allen, and the committee is asked to scrutinize it in every way, and especially to note the respects in which Allen, by his testimony, exposes himself to contradiction if he is false.

The narrative of this witness is briefly as follows:

He was, in January and February, 1865, with his partners, engaged, in New York, in the recruit and bounty brokerage business. He was applied to by Colonel L. C. Baker, who came as the confidential representative of General Fry, to aid him in breaking up frauds in recruiting. Much negotiation ensued and Colonel Baker entered into an arrangement with him, which General Fry was, by Baker, pledged to carry out. The witness was fully cross-examined by the counsel for General Fry and in the presence of General Fry, as to the terms of this understanding, so as to lay the foundation for a contradiction, and the form of the examination clearly implied that such was its purpose. The witness stated that Colonel Baker agreed that "jumpers" should be credited and the credits sold for the highest price, and went minutely into the conditions which Colonel Baker made in advance of Allen's seeing General Fry personally. It was vital to contradict him in these particulars if possible, because, as he testified that he related them to General Fry in their first interview, it would have destroyed the witness utterly to impeach the foundation of his story. The form of asking for a summons from Colonel L. C. Baker was gone through with, and although it appeared in the testimony that Colonel Baker was in the city of Washington at the time, it is impossible not to notice, in passing, that we have not seen him upon the stand.

But continuing the narrative, Allen testifies that, on a day which he fixes, Colonel Baker came to him saying that General Fry wanted to see him in Washington. Here is a fact which requires us to pause a moment. I say *fact*, because if it were not a fact, Colonel Baker would certainly have been called to disprove it. Why did General Fry want to see Allen? Baker was constantly passing to and fro between Washington and New York, and he and General Fry kept the wires vibrating with interchanges of thought. General Fry knew from Baker what had occurred, and what had been agreed upon with Allen. If Baker had not told him, Baker could have told him fully as to all that. But he wanted to see Allen in person, and Allen went to Washington.

He says General Fry received him very cordially, and requested two persons whom he found in the room to leave them in privacy. Is this statement true? It is not denied that Allen came to Washington to see General Fry, that he did see him, and at his office in the War Department. Did he see him alone? If not, where is the person who was present? No suggestion was made to the witness on his cross-examination that any one was present, but a young man is brought from Philadelphia to swear that he was the clerk of General Fry, and that he was not present when Allen was, and was not one of those asked to leave the room. De Corsa is this gentleman's name, and his identification with General Fry is suggestive of the "Corsican Brothers." Does he prove anything, however, which in the remotest way militates with what Allen says?

Allen states that a full talk was had between himself and General Fry at the time in question, in which talk it was agreed that sham enlistments should be made, that credits for these enlistments should be given, and that these credits should be sold for whatever they would bring, and the profits of the operation should go—not into the treasury, certainly.

A satisfactory understanding having been reached, the parties separated after arranging some details. Allen requested, he says, that Colonel Ilges should be selected as mustering officer, as he had mustered for his (Allen's) firm before, and that an order should be made as to the credits which among other things should remove an impediment likely otherwise to be found in the fact that Colonel Ilges was a regular army officer, and not, therefore, authorized to act in connexion with the provost marshal, or the provost marshal in connexion with him, in allowing credits. This, he says, General Fry agreed to do, and we know it was done. (See order.) Allen returned to New York, and at once set about his labors.

He says that after his doings at Hoboken had culminated, as I have previously related, and about the 16th or 17th of March, General Fry telegraphed to New York that he wanted to see him (Allen) again. Here is another very exposed point. Allen says Colonel Baker saw the despatch, and, besides, files and records are kept; and the date being fixed by Allen, if such a despatch was not sent, the operator at either end of the line could contradict him. He came at once to Washington, and the train being delayed he reached the War Department, as he says, after business hours. Being denied entrance to the War Department and to General Fry, he told the doorkeeper that if General Fry knew he was there he would see him, and sent in his card. As he predicted, this gained him an audience instantly. He says General Fry saw him in his room alone, having signified his wish to be private. But Mr. De Corsa doesn't remember being there when this happened. He says he didn't see Allen then at all. Is it denied that Allen was there, and there at that time, and had a private interview with General Fry, and on the subject which Allen says was the subject between them? Is any part of this denied? If it is *not*, why go through the parade of calling Mr. De Corsa from Philadelphia? If it *is* denied, the denial is shown to be false, as we shall presently see by evidence, documentary and otherwise, which puts it beyond all question.

The committee is asked to read the whole of this interview as detailed by the witness, between the almost incessant interruptions and contests over the form and technicalities of the questions put to him, by which a day was consumed. Its attentive, searching reading will reveal many tests of its truth in connexion with other evidence.

Allen says he reminded General Fry that he had come in answer to his despatch. General Fry said yes, and at once referred to the Hoboken matter. General Fry presently inquired " *what had become of the money?*" Allen said he had over $60,000 of it. General Fry then inquired, *what he was going to do with it!* Allen said he was going to keep it, according to their previous agreement. General Fry then inquired *if Baker had not asked for some of it!*

Allen, soon after this, explained that there was $54,000 more in Colonel Ilges's hands, which his firm had been compelled to pay in, as heretofore explained, and that he wanted an order for it from him (General Fry,) as he could not get it without.

Suggestive as the interview had been up to this point, when we consider the circumstances and the parties to it, it here became still more significant. General Fry, the witness says, approached him, putting his hands on his shoulders, and with a spirit and manner which may be better inferred from what followed than described, he proceeded to ply him with the very lechery of persuasion. He informed the witness that what he wished most to talk with him about, and what he sent for him for, was a matter at Utica, and this he proceeded to explain. He told him that he wanted evidence which would convict Captain Crandall of fraud, and which would fasten some imputation upon me (Mr. Conkling;) this was the point he labored. Allen told him that from his information he believed that the facts at Utica would point to Haddock as the guilty party, and not to Crandall. To this General Fry at once replied that he did not want evidence against Haddock, but against Crandall, and that he wanted something " *at all hazards*" which would implicate me (Mr. Conkling;) that I had set myself up as a champion of Crandall, &c., &c., and that he wanted to find something against me. He told the witness that he knew *he* could do it, and he did not know any other man who could; that he would not trust any of Baker's men, &c., &c., and that he must go to Utica and do what he wanted; and if he would he (General Fry) would make an order while he was gone directing the $54,000 to be paid over to him. After some further conversation, Allen said he would see what he could do. He then told General Fry that the order had better be to pay the money back to the party who paid it, as Riley was the cashier of the concern and had paid it to Ilges, and was the one to receive it.

The interview closed with further and repeated injunctions by General Fry to obtain the desired evidence, and assurances that the order should be made. Allen returned to New York, and, as he says, disclosed to four persons, who are named, what had transpired between himself and General Fry. I could not call these persons to testify to what Allen told them; the rules of evidence would not allow it; but General Fry could have called them, and would have done so if they could have contradicted Allen.

The committee, however, permitted some things to be proved by Allen and others as to what followed this interview of March 18.

Allen and the four persons to whom he revealed the interview with General Fry held frequent consultations as to what course to pursue, and as the result of these consultations, the following plan was hit upon :

Allen did not go to Utica, but waited quietly for five days, visiting Albany meanwhile, and at the end of this time, and on the 24th of March, a sufficient space having elapsed to have enabled him to go to Utica, a despatch was written to General Fry by one of the four persons in the secret, signed by Allen, and sent to General Fry. Here is the original despatch :

> "ASTOR HOUSE, NEW YORK, *March* 24, 1865.
>
> "Brigadier General FRY,
>
> "*Provost Marshal General, Washington, D. C.*
>
> "*I have just returned from Utica, and Colonel Ilges refuses to deliver the money received from me because your order is dated the 11th instead of 10th March. Please answer through Colonel Baker.*
>
> "THEO. ALLEN."

We shall see in a moment what order these dates referred to; but first let us follow the sequence of events.

This despatch did all that its authors contrived it to do, and in a few hours the desired answer came, "through Colonel Baker," as requested. Here it is :

> "WAR DEPARTMENT, PROVOST MARSHAL GENERAL'S BUREAU,
>
> "*Washington, D. C., March* 24, 1865.
>
> "I have been informed by Theodore Allen, of New York, that Colonel Ilges declines to turn over the money received from the bounty jumpers, as directed by me, on the 11th instant. *I wish you to see Colonel Ilges and have him turn over this money as directed.*
>
> "JAMES B. FRY,
>
> "*Provost Marshal General.*
>
> "Colonel L. C. BAKER,
>
> "*No. 12 Vesey Street, New York.*"

Baker took this despatch to Colonel Ilges, and he went, with Allen and his partners to the Broadway National Bank and there made a check, payable to Allen's firm, for $54,000, and the money was paid over on the spot. (See check copied in report of Colonel Ilges.)

Speaking as this transaction is, in its fixed and unmistakable features, and positively as it is sworn to, it is just to General Fry that the committee should require Allen to be fortified. Partly for this reason and partly to put upon General Fry a necessity to submit himself to examination, which it seemed to me he could not disregard. I offered in evidence, in connexion with the testimony of Allen, the testimony of Edward Maloy, who corroborated every statement which the rules of law and the objections made by the counsel for General Fry would permit me to inquire into. I offered also certain despatches from General Fry, which may be referred to here as well as anywhere. The first is as follows :

"PROVOST MARSHAL GENERAL'S BUREAU,
"*Washington, D. C., March* 18, 1866.
"Colonel L. C. BAKER, *No.* 12 *Vesey Street, New York.*

"*Allen is here, and tells me he can provide information about the Utica district. I have told him to do so. He starts back to New York to-night, and will see you. Produce all the facts in the case.*

"JAMES B. FRY,
"*Provost Marshal General.*"

It will be seen that this despatch proves beyond cavil that Allen was in Washington at the time he says he was; that he had a conference with General Fry on the subject of "*providing*" information about the Utica district.

The committee is asked in the light of this despatch, and in the absence of all explanation, and with General Fry declining to trust himself upon the witness stand, what General Fry summoned Allen to Washington for, and how he came to be in confidential intercourse with him about "*providing*" information in regard to Utica?

How came Allen to "tell" him he could "*provide*" such evidence? A few other questions as to this mysterious interview may test Allen's truthfulness. What honest use had General Fry for Allen in such a connexion? He had Haddock and his corps of detectives and messengers; and he knew that Haddock's salvation depended upon shifting from his own shoulders to Captain Crandall's, the guilt which must rest somewhere for what had been done and attempted at Utica. It was certain, therefore, that Haddock would leave no evidence unfound. General Fry had Colonel Baker and his emissaries also at his beck and nod. He had them actually at that very time on the scent, as the evidence shows, to hunt up something at Utica. Carlile and Gall had been to Utica already, as he knew; so had Maloy; all being picked detectives. Besides all this, General Fry had at this time selected an officer, Major Luddington, to go to Utica. He had procured him to be detailed, subject to his "verbal instructions," and Luddington had been despatched to Utica, and Baker had been telegraphed to help him.

All this machinery was in General Fry's hands; all of it had been set in motion against Crandall; nothing had been done toward investigating Haddock, though proofs and accusations against him lay in piles before General Fry; and yet Theodore Allen, in addition, is telegraphed to Washington to "*provide*" information as to the Utica district.

Was this interview with Allen on March 18 a private one? If it was not, who is the man who witnessed it? If it was private, what was the occasion of privacy? Did General Fry have any private or public business with Allen at that time which he is willing to explain? Was any suggested on Allen's cross-examination? Did he make any record of his business with Allen on that day?

It must not be forgotten that the counsel for General Fry, with General Fry present and prompting him, in his questions to Allen, on cross-examination, as to the interview of March 18, pointedly assumed that the $54,000 was a subject of discussion.

Look at another despatch sent the day after General Fry believed Allen had been to Utica, the day after he made the order to pay him $54,000 :

"PROVOST MARSHAL GENERAL'S BUREAU,
"*Washington, D. C., March* 25, 1865.
"Colonel L. C. BAKER, *New York :*

"*You must prepare all the facts in the case of the Utica district without reference to Major Luddington's report. It is absolutely necessary for me to*

*hare them, whether Major Luddington has been able to obtain them or not.
See Allen and let him make it his business to straighten this matter out.*

"**JAMES B. FRY,**
"*Provost Marshal General.*"

This despatch is ten days after Baker had telegraphed General Fry—
"*I have discovered extensive and astounding enlistment frauds at Elmira,
New York. I am well satisfied that Major Haddock is a party indirectly con-
nected with these frauds,*" &c.

Yet no anxiety is felt to explore Haddock, but General Fry is in frenzied
pursuit of an object at Utica. The committee will find food for reflection here.

In further corroboration of Allen's statement is an order to Ilges, dated
March 19, the day after Allen's second interview with General Fry, in which
Ilges is ordered to pay over the money received in connexion with the "jumpers," and saying that the credits are to be *disallowed.* If the committee can
discover any relief for General Fry, in the fact that, in addition to all his other
acts, he proposed to deprive Jersey City of the credits for which the money had
been honestly paid, and paid in consequence of his own plan and his own orders,
he will, no doubt, receive the full benefit of the fact. I am not able to suggest
any argument to be derived from it, except one which sinks General Fry still
lower as an officer and a man.

It may be argued that General Fry acted in ignorance of some fact in order-
ing Colonel Ilges to pay the money to Allen's firm. It may even be insisted
that General Fry did not know to whom it was to go; that he may have supposed it was advanced by the authorities of Jersey City, and would go back to
them. To show that all this would be an afterthought if suggested, as it is
fair to the counsel for General Fry to remember that it has not been, and also to
sustain Allen, I refer to the report of Colonel Ilges, and to the letters to and from
General Fry, which there appear. It will be seen that every fact was brought home
to General Fry's knowledge; that the action of General Fry shocked and confounded this officer; that he obeyed orders under protest, and delayed obedience till he
could confer with General Fry by letter, and that he actually proceeded to
Washington and laid the case in person before him, and that General Fry ordered the money paid to Allen, Riley, and Hughes, after all this.

The following passages in this report are commended to the attention of the
committee.

It will be seen that they corroborate Allen thoroughly, and render yet more
clear the guilt of General Fry.

Extract from the statement of Lieutenant Colonel Ilges.

"Messrs. Allen, Riley, and Hughes furnished the recruits with the local
bounty. The amount was established by me as three hundred dollars, this being the amount of bounty paid elsewhere. These gentlemen were permitted at
and admitted to my office for the following reasons:

"I. They came to me through Colonel Baker. They were recommended to
me as the instruments of, and in the confidence of, the government.

"II. They produced to me a document showing that they were the representatives of the city of Hoboken, New Jersey, the said document being a contract
between them and the city council of Hoboken to fill the quota of said city.

"III. They furnished me with a copy of the following telegraphic despatch, viz:

"'WAR DEPARTMENT, PROVOST MARSHAL GENERAL'S BUREAU,
"'*Washington, D. C., March 5, 1865.*

('"Original by telegraph.)

"'Captain HARRY J. MILLS, *Provost Marshal, Newark, New Jersey.*

"'Until otherwise ordered, you are directed to allow credits for such men as
Brevet Lieutenant Colonel Guido Ilges, captain 14th United States infantry,

certifies to you are enlisted by him. He is recruiting at Hoboken. Inform Colonel Ely of this order. *The case is special and confidential.*

"'JAMES B. FRY,
"'*Provost Marshal General.*'

"In order to muster in volunteers, as I was instructed to do, I had to obtain the money to be paid to them as bounty and to brokers as hand money from some quarter, and these three men came to me with the sanction and in the confidence of the authorities, and as proper representatives of certain localities. Therefore I felt justified, and still feel so, under the then existing circumstances, that I was then doing right and endeavoring to promote the interests of the government. Besides, Colonel Baker was fully aware of the manner in which the business of my office was transacted, as in conversations with him at different times I informed him of everything in connexion with my office. On the 10th day of March, 1865, when the aforementioned one hundred and eighty-three bounty-jumpers were mustered in by me and kept by me in confinement, and also on the following day, I hesitated and declined to credit these men to any of the localities; but upon consideration and the re-reading of the order received in regard to credits, (copies of which are given with this report and made a portion thereof,) and when the mayor of the city of Jersey City informed me that Colonel Baker had assured him that the credits allowed by me are "all right," I concluded to pursue the following course:

"To take charge of the $300 bounty money of each one of these 183 recruits and to deposit the same in National bank, subject to the order of the Provost Marshal General.

"I considered it my duty under the then existing orders regulating the mustering service, that the bounty money of each one of the 183 recruits should either be paid into their own hands, or should be deposited and in my own hand at all events, that this money should actually be paid by the parties who received the credits.

"I thought then, and still think, that these men, if they were to be kept in the service without being proven deserters of other military organizations before their enlistment with me, were fully entitled to the amount of local bounty; but that if they were proven deserters, the United States treasury should be the recipient of this money.

"Messrs. Allen, Riley and Hughes accordingly paid into my hands the sum of $54,000, this being the amount of bounty claimed by me as due to 180 recruits. The said party were to pay into my hands the sum of $900 more, for the remaining three recruits; but they failed to do so, telling me, upon my repeated application for this amount, that it was not necessary for them to do so, *as the amount in my hands ($54,000) would be paid back to them within a few days by order of the Provost Marshal General.* This amount (54,000) was deposited by me in the Broadway National Bank, March 15, 1866.

"I immediately wrote to the Provost Marshal General at Washington, D. C., asking for instruction whether to pay this amount to the recruits then in confinement, or to the commanding officer at Fort Lafayette, who had charge of these men, or whether I should turn it into the United States treasury. In reply to this letter I received, on the 20th of March, the following communication:

"'WAR DEPARTMENT, PROVOST MARSHAL GENERAL'S OFFICE.
"'*Washington, D. C., March 19, 1865.*

"'COLONEL: I am directed by the Provost Marshal General to inform you that the credits of the men mustered by you March 11, 1865, at Hoboken, New

Jersey, and credited to Jersey City at large, are disallowed, *and that you will refund the money to the parties who advanced it.*

"'I am, colonel, very respectfully, your obedient servant,

"'W. OWENS,

"'*Captain 6th United States Cavalry, A. A. A. G.*

"'Brevet Lieut. Col. GUIDO ILGES, U. S. A.

"'*Mustering Officer Hoboken, New Jersey.*

"'*Thinking that the Provost Marshall General might not fully understand this whole matter, I deemed it my duty to write to him the following communication in explanation before paying back the money, viz:*

"'RECRUITING SERVICE, 14TH INFANTRY,

"'163 *Hester street, New York city, March 21, 1865.*

"'CAPTAIN: I have the honor to acknowledge the receipt of your communication of March 19, 1865, informing me that the credits of men mustered by me March 11, 1865, at Hoboken, New Jersey, and credited to Jersey City at large, are disallowed, and instructing me to refund this money to the parties who advanced it.

"'I beg leave to state that no men were mustered by me on the aforesaid date, but I infer that this communication meant to say the 10th instead of the 11th of March, 1863.

"'I would respectfully state that on the said day four regulars were mustered by me, and that if their credits are not to be effected they should be excluded in the order. I mustered on the 10th day of March one hundred and eighty-three volunteers for three years, so-called bounty-jumpers, and they were credited to Jersey City at large, with the exception of fifteen recruits that were credited to Clinton township, Essex county, fourth congressional district, New Jersey.

"'I would further state that I have at my disposal $300 local bounty for each of these one hundred and eighty-three recruits, *and that I received this amount from Allen, Riley & Co., who had contracted with the counties for these credits;* and I would, therefore, respectfully request that you inform me *whether or not I am to refund this money to these parties, or to the proper representatives of the places who received the credits.*

"'These one hundred and eighty-three recruits were properly mustered into the service by me, and I credited them according to instructions and orders regulating the mustering service. None of these recruits have as yet been proven to have been credited before; and when I gave these credits I did so as a United States officer, believing that I was doing my duty, and advancing the interests of the plan of Colonel Baker, sanctioned by the Provost Marshal General. I am informed that the county representatives who received these credits paid a large amount of premiums to Messrs. Allen, Riley & Co. besides the $300 local bounty; and as they have done so after having been informed by me of the correctness of these credits, I would respectfully call your attention to the fact that when these credits are disallowed the said localities will lose a large amount of money paid out by them in good faith. I am not aware what amount of money was paid to Messrs. Allen, Riley & Co. for each recruit, and cannot even give a probable guess, as I only collected the usual amount from them—$300 for each recruit, this being the amount of bounty paid to a recruit enlisted at Hoboken, New Jersey.

"'I would here add that Messrs. Allen, Riley & Co. are the parties who carried out the plan above referred to, and I only allowed them to be present in my office, and to contract for these credits contrary to existing orders, after I had been assured by Colonel L. C. Baker, special agent of the War Department, that the whole proceeding was sanctioned by the Provost Marshal General United States army.

"'I therefore respectfully request that you inform me, at your earliest convenience, what disposition I am to make of the money referred to.

"'I remain, captain, very respectfully, your obedient servant,

"'GUIDO ILGES,

"' Capt. 14th Infantry, Brevet Lieut. Col. Vols., Recruiting Officer.

'"Captain W. OWENS,

"'5th U. S. Cavalry, A. A. A. G., Washington, D. C.'

"In reply to this letter of the 21st I received on the 24th of the same month the following reply:

"'WAR DEPARTMENT, PROVOST MARSHAL GENERAL'S BUREAU,

"'Washington, D. C., March 23, 1865.

"'COLONEL: I have the honor to acknowledge the receipt of your communif cation of the 21st instant, and, in reply, would state that the communication o- the 19th instant, referred to, was intended to cover the cases of the 183 so-called bounty-jumpers, and that the amount which you received for the purpose of paying bounties to these 183 so-called bounty-jumpers the Provost Marshal directs to be refunded to the parties who advanced it.

"'I am, colonel, very respectfully, your obedient servant,

"'W. OWENS,

"' Captain 5th U. S. cavalry, A. A. A. G.

"'Brevet Lieut. Colonel GUIDO ILGIS,

"' United States army, Hester street, New York.'

"Messrs. Allen, Riley and Hughes, in company with the aforesaid Mr. Stanley, called upon me on the 24th of March, and they (seeming aware of the foregoing order) demanded of me the $54,000, and, upon my refusal to give up the money to them until I could see Colonel L. C. Baker and ask his advice in the matter, they informed me that legal proceedings would be forthwith instituted in order to compel me to give up to them their money. I immediately called upon Colonel L. C. Baker at his office, but being unable to see him then; I proceeded to the office of the United States district attorney, D. L. Smith, No. 12 Chambers street, and laid my case before one of the attorneys of his office, who advised me not to give up the money until I had further orders from Washington. I also called upon several other regular army officers of the city, and was by them advised to the same effect.

" On the 25th of March, 1865, I was again sent for by Colonel L. C. Baker, and upon my arrival at his office I was shown by him a telegraphic despatch from the Provost Marshal General to him, directing him to order me to turn over the amount of money ($54,000) held by me as bounty for these 183 so-called bounty-jumpers, to Messrs. Allen, Riley & Co.

"After hesitating and waiting nearly one hour at Colonel Baker's office, I proceeded to the National Broadway Bank, accompanied by Messrs. Allen, Riley, Hughes and Stanly, and there drew the following check, viz:

"'No. 24. NEW YORK, March 25, 1865.

"' National Broadway Bank. pay to Messrs. Peter Riley & Co., or beare-. fifty-four thousand dollars.

"'$54,000.

"'GUIDO ILGES,

"' Capt. 14th U. S. Inf., Brevet Lieut. Col. U. S. A.,

"'Recruiting Officer.''

" Which check I handed to Mr. Peter Riley in presence of the aforesaid gentlemen, who presented the same to the paying teller at the said bank, and received $54,000 in national currency therefor.

" It is also proper for me to state that on the 17th of March, having received permission, I proceeded to Washington city, *and in person related to the Provost Marshal General United States army all the details connected with the office at Hoboken, the capture of these* 183 *so-called bounty-jumpers, and the amount of money in my hands;* asking at the same time for instructions in regard to the disposal of this money; to which he replied that further orders would be sent to me by mail. I expressed to him my fear that at some future day I might be called upon for explanations why I had at my office at Hoboken acted contrary to existing orders and regulations governing the mustering service, *and that I intended to ask for a court of inquiry, when the Provost Marshal General assured me that I had done my duty well, and only obeyed orders.*"

What answer does General Fry make to all this evidence, direct and circumstantial, oral and documentary ? He attempts to impeach the general character for truth of Theodore Allen. We shall see, if we have not seen already in the argument, that Theodore Allen is only one of the rivets fastening the evidence, and that if we were to drop him altogether from the case General Fry would still be hopelessly entangled.

But as all parts of the evidence should be fairly weighed, let us examine the attempted impeachment, and while we do so let us forget how far-fetched such evidence was, compared with other kinds of proof at once accessible and effectual against Allen, if Allen testified untruly. When this witness was introduced to the committee-room it could not be, or rather it was not, disguised that the counsel for General Fry was somewhat nonplused. No sooner was the general nature of his testimony apparent than motions for delay began. Various reasons were assigned for a postponement of the examination of the witness, and at last the day was worn out in these repeated efforts on behalf of General Fry. But before the sitting ended there was entered on the record a full notice in substance of what the witness was relied upon to prove. After this, an entire week elapsed before General Fry was compelled to proceed with his evidence in reply; so that very ample time was allowed to collect impeaching testimony.

The result is before the committee. Three witnesses from New York were asked for. One of these, Mr. Kennedy, superintendent of police, was afterwards stopped in coming, it seems, on the application of the counsel of General Fry to a member of the committee. It subsequently dropped out, on the examination of Carpenter, that Mr. Kennedy knew Allen well, and had been heard to speak of his character, but not in the direction desired by General Fry.

But Carpenter and Pettey came. It is enough to say of Carpenter that he on the stand confessed that after being applied to some three days previous to the day on which he delivered his testimony, he went around to see if he could find some one who would speak against Allen, in order that he might refer to them as the persons whom he had heard speak against him. He said he knew it was customary to ask witnesses whether they had heard others speak against the witness to be impeached, and he intended to qualify himself before he started. It only remains to say of this witness, that he further stated that he disclosed his testimony to General Fry in person, before being called to the stand. There was, therefore, no surprise about his testimony, and no mistake about the act of advisedly bringing the witness forward.

Mr. Pettey was not asked whether he would believe Allen on his oath, although attention was called at the time to the omission.

General Fry next called a policeman who has lived in Washington five years, and knew Allen seven years ago. This was the third witness, and was produced after a personal interview with General Fry. He, also, was not asked whether he would believe Allen, although he was called for the purpose of being so asked, as we were given to understand.

The fourth and last witness was a young officer who never lived in New York, but served at that place on the staff of General Dix for a large part of a year. He had heard comments by other members of the staff upon Allen in regard to recruiting, and nothing else. The witness, without being asked whether or not he would believe Allen, was allowed to close the procession, four in number, of impeaching witnesses. It is not too much to say, when the nature of the testimony given by Allen is borne in mind, and also his admitted relationship toward General Fry, and his avowed connexion with the Hoboken transaction, that the idea of withholding both Generals Fry and Baker as witnesses, and at the same time making a labored effort at attacking the general character of the witness, is a display of tactics almost, if not altogether, grotesque. It is a Chinese warfare. But when we compare the performance with the advertisement, it awakens renewed wonder that General Fry should not have felt able to brave the dangers of giving testimony himself of matters known to him better than to any one else, and which call so loudly for explanation or denial.

The expedient of endeavoring to distract attention from the absence of the evidence for which instinct and reason alike cried out, if indeed Allen were untruthful, was rendered the more sorry by the appearance of nine or ten well-known, respectable citizens of New York, including a member of the House, who fully sustained the witness and overthrew entirely the faintly attempted impeachment.

I propose now to examine in some of the more obvious aspects of the case the question whether the testimony, of which the statement of Theodore Allen is a part, is true.

In order to do this, we must first see what weight of testimony is requisite to establish the alleged fact; then what can be learned from the probabilities independent of the testimony to be tested; then how far the evidence is corroborated directly, and thus we shall arrive at the value of the evidence and at the truth of the matter.

First. As to the force the testimony must have to produce conviction.

What is it that makes us require evidence of guilt? The presumption of innocence. What is that? It is faith or belief that the person is incapable of the crime.

Does that presumption still exist in this case? Does it continue in spite of the evidence as to matters distinct from the New Jersey affair?

What is the philosophy of the maxim, "*Falsus in uno, falsus in omnibus?*" Is it not simply, that after the absence of integrity is once established, no proof is necessary to establish it again? Apply that principle to the facts before us. Here is a man confessedly capable of deliberate and malicious falsehood; capable of violating the first principles of honor; capable of disregarding the cardinal virtue of his profession; capable of violating the professional and official obligations by which he is bound; capable of violating the privileges of Congress, and of aspersing his superior officers; capable of blackening private character from motives of revenge; capable of endeavoring to present evidence to substantiate allegations which he does not believe; capable of sitting down under proof against him utterly destructive of his character, which, if false, he could explode at once by his own testimony, and willing to assume the position that if compelled to testify it shall be with the understanding that he shall not be impeached or contradicted.

What presumption of innocence remains in such a case?

Second. What probabilities are there, independent of the evidence in question, from which we can judge of what is likely to be true?

The case abounds in evidence that General Fry had a most determined, and, indeed, violent feeling toward the people of my district, toward the provost marshal, and especially against me. He was resolved to discipline us all with great severity. In addition to this, he was zealous and headlong in his partisanship of Haddock. Mr. Dana testifies that even as late as April 3 he stigmatized as corrupt all those who imputed blame to Haddock. Previous to the 18th of March General Fry knew that I had charged Haddock with the frauds which he (General Fry) was seeking to fasten upon Captain Crandall. He was, as the event has shown, intensely angered. His bridled emotion, described by Mr. Dana, proves this, and it appears in various ways that he had put himself upon destroying Crandall and sustaining Haddock.

With what we know now of the lengths to which General Fry's revenge will carry him, is it probable or improbable that he was at the time in question longing for some weapon to use against me? This is a very pregnant question in considering the naturalness or unnaturalness of Allen's story.

If General Fry was, at the time referred to, in quest of something which might aid him against me, was Theodore Allen a man whom he would have been likely to trust on such an errand? This also is an important question.

Who was Theodore Allen? He was a man of address, of nerve, of talent, and he knew men. He had been selected by Generals Baker and Fry as the shrewdest and aptest man who could be found in the city of New York, both for dis-. coveries and concealments. It was in this character that General Fry knew him

General Fry had once confided in him, so much as to put himself far into his power, and to show that he trusted him. Look for proof of this at the admitted facts of the Hoboken affair.

Moreover, Allen was largely in General Fry's power. Sixty-six thousand dollars, less the expenses, had already been realized from a very questionable transaction, to say the least, with which both were connected. Fifty-four thousand more depended on the favor or the exactions of General Fry. Moreover General Fry had the power to order his arrest at any moment, as he afterwards did when he found Allen had failed to gratify his revengeful intention to manufacture evidence. In these circumstances was Allen the man he would trust or not? General Fry's counsel says he never had seen him but twice, and he was too much of a stranger to be selected for such a purpose. Experience and human nature are opposed to this idea. It is not the rule for men in power to select those they have known long, and who have known them well, for employments which are awkward to talk about.

A second interview seems rather a nick of time for such a purpose.

It was at the second interview that Macbeth proposed Banquo's murder to the man he thought might do the work, and it happened also that he requested the attendants to leave the room.

Is it not even possible, I suggest to the counsel, that Allen may have plagarized this and other examples, deemed true to nature by the great masters of the human heart?

At this point let me ask, What is the precise presumption left to be overcome by Allen's testimony? Is it the presumption that General Fry was incapable of making use of unfair means against a man he hated, or is it the presumption that General Fry would not have selected Theodore Allen?

Now, let us turn to Allen's testimony for a moment. What part of it stands alone?

Is he not corroborated in nearly every particular? Is he contradicted in any one particular?

I will speak only of the one point in his testimony most vital, and of course most contested in argument, to wit: The statement that General Fry proposed to him to go to Utica and find something, at all hazards, which would fasten imputation upon me, and that upon a compliance with this request, hinged the $54,000.

The despatch sent by General Fry to Colonel Baker March 18, already referred to, proves four things beyond all question : *First*, that Allen was in Washington that day ; *second*, that he had an interview with General Fry ; *third*, that in that interview the subject of getting evidence at Utica was talked of; and *fourth*, that Allen undertook to *provide* information.

About this same time, indeed only the day before, we find General Fry, in another despatch to Colonel Baker, expressing his great anxiety to procure evidence from Utica, and mentioning in a hostile manner that I, (Mr. Conkling,) " deny Crandall's corruption." The committee cannot fail to see the coincidence here again between this despatch and Allen's testimony.

We find that Allen goes back to New York, and that after a disclosure by him to them of what had occurred, he and his confidential advisers are in daily consultation, until that consultation ends in sending a despatch to General Fry in Allen's name.

The committee is asked to examine this despatch, and see if it is explainable in any way except as Allen's testimony explains it. Why did he telegraph General Fry, " *I have just returned from Utica !*" If going to Utica had nothing to do with the $54,000, it would have been very strange to put it in a despatch and pay for its going over the wires to General Fry. This would have been very strange, even if Allen had *in truth been to Utica ;* but how much more strange it would be, when he had *not been to Utica*, to telegraph that he had been, if there was no connexion between going to Utica and getting an order for the $54,000. Could anything be more speaking !

Why did Allen wait five days before sending this despatch if it was not to allow time to have gone to Utica ?

Why did General Fry forthwith send back by telegraph an order for the $54,000 ?

Why did General Fry on the next day telegraph Baker to commit the Utica matter to Allen ?

When these things can be explained away, it will be time to inquire why Theodore Allen, without motive, unless his statement is true, should come here to confront a man in official station, who would have dared in return to confront him, but that " conscience does make cowards of us all."

In conclusion, I have only to say that whenever the committee shall be prepared to receive it, I shall be ready to point out evidence substantiating all statements made by me as to the administration of the bureau of General Fry

---

MEMORANDUM OF LAW SUBMITTED IN CONNEXION WITH THE FOREGOING ARGUMENT.

General Fry has, by his counsel, submitted to the committee an elaborate argument to show that there is a technical impediment in the way of a representative elect conducting a criminal prosecution for the United States before a military court.

The position assumed is, that though applied to, and appealed to, by the government to render it professional service, though the occasion is such that no other citizen would be justified in refusing, and though special circumstances may render it important, as Mr. Stanton testifies was the case in this instance, that a particular person, rather than some other, should act, yet these considerations ought not to govern if the person thus applied to is a representative elect to Congress.

The suggestion is that such a professional employment constitutes " holding an office," and that by law there is an incompatibility in the case.

The counsel for General Fry virtually concedes that no statute upholds this view, and he rests his argument upon the Constitution.

It is submitted that this position is as unsound in law as it is in morals, patriotism, and common sense, and it is insisted that a representative elect is, in such a case, precisely in the same position, technically and substantially, as any other citizen.

It is believed that the legislation of the country can hardly involve such absurdities as would result from the doctrine expounded by General Fry.

It cannot be true that a lawyer, by being elected to Congress, thereby loses his right to practice his profession. Nor is it true that the government is under any disability which prevents its exercising the right of every other litigant to select the attorney or counsel who in the particular case is most likely to be useful. Nor is it true that though a representative or representative elect may properly act as counsel for any and every other client, he may not so act for his government. It may be asserted with some confidence that no such folly has been committed as to allow members of Congress to act as counsel *against* the government, as it is admitted by all they properly may, and at the same time to prohibit their acting *for* the government, or in its aid.

I.

The provision of the Constitution referred to (Sec. VI, of Art. I) has no application to the case. The language is, "no person holding an office under the United States shall be a member of either house during his continuance in office." For several reasons this language has no application to the facts before the committee. One reason will suffice, viz: that the act of prosecuting Haddock before a court-martial in no sense constituted "holding any office under the United States." If this be so, there is, of course, an end of the argument, and there would have been an end of it, even if Haddock had been prosecuted, not by a representative elect, but by a representative after he had qualified as such.

1. The office of judge advocate exists, and is, of course, created by law. It is a well-defined office, as much so as the office of district attorney or marshal or collector of internal revenue. (See 12 Statutes at Large, p. 598; 2 Brightley's Digest, p. 25.) A judge advocate can be appointed in only one way, (except the temporary appointment during vacation of the Senate,) viz: "by the President, by and with the advice and consent of the Senate." The President must nominate to the Senate, and the Senate must confirm, and then a commission issues to the appointee. (See same statute.) Judge advocates have the *rank, pay, and emoluments of a major of cavalry.* (See the same statute.) This gives a salary as well as military rank.

2. It need hardly be argued that no "*office under the United States*" can exist unless it is created by the Constitution or by act of Congress. It follows, then, that the office of judge advocate exists only under the statute already cited, because no other statute now exists and none other did exist in 1865 by which such an office is created, and it is not created by the Constitution. We know, therefore, exactly what the office of judge advocate is, and also its character, mode of appointment, tenure, and compensation. Is there any pretence that this office was conferred in the case before the committee? There was no nomination to the Senate, no appointment by the President, and no commission whatever.

3. But it is said the Haddock court-martial should have had a regular official judge advocate, and an argument is deduced from this that it did have one. The point was raised on the trial of Haddock that the law required an official judge advocate, duly appointed, &c. This point was overruled, and properly so, as all the statutes on the subject expressly authorize persons *not* judge advocates to act as such on trials, and Mr. Stanton testifies that during his administration, in a majority of important military trials, the prosecution has

been conducted, not by those holding the office of judge advocate, but by counsel employed for the particular trial.

4. It is still further suggested, however, that whoever is assigned to act as judge advocate, and does act as a judge advocate, would, if he were present, thereby actually becomes "judge advocate," and holds an "office." This would seem a violent assumption, even if it depended upon general reasoning; but, in addition to this, several acts of Congress preclude the idea altogether.

a. Several acts of Congress provide that no man shall enter upon any office without taking an official oath. This is universal, and the oath is prescribed in so many words. Recent statutes prescribe an additional oath of office, without taking which no man can hold an office.

Does any statute require these oaths to be taken by one who merely appears to try a criminal before a military court? Are these oaths, in fact, taken by one who merely thus appears? Was any such oath taken in the case in hand?

Every "judge advocate" must take, and does take, these oaths before he can become "judge advocate," but he does not take them because he appears, nor when he appears, before a military court.

No official oath is taken by anybody in organizing a military court. The "judge advocate," if there is one, if not, the person officiating for him, the stenographer, and the members of the court, all swear not to disclose the proceedings, &c., but will any one pretend that in thus swearing, they all install themselves in "office?"

b. The statutes regulating courts-martial (see act of 1806, 1 Brightley's Dig., 80) leave no room for argument as to the effect and nature of the oath prescribed as a part of the proceedings. The provision is as follows: "The judge advocate, *or person officiating as such*," shall take the following oath: (The oath is simply not to disclose the proceedings improperly.)

This is the only oath required, and it is to be taken as much by a judge advocate, as by a counsellor who casually acts, and so *vice versa*.

Is this an oath of office? If so, what is the sense of its being administered to judge advocates who have already taken the oath of office?

Do those who take this oath thereby take upon themselves an office? If so, the judge advocate, and all the members of the court, would necessarily acquire each a second office, because all the members of the court take the same oath substantially. The statement of the proposition shows its absurdity. The oath is of the same nature as that taken by a grand juror, and no more constitutes swearing into office than does the oath taken by Odd-Fellows, or Masons, or members of any other body, whether established by law or not, whose doings are private.

c. It is suggested that the order assembling the court-martial, and naming those who compose it, confers an appointment to office, or constitutes an appointment to office. This idea can be so readily tested that argument cannot be necessary.

In the first place, courts-martial are not ordered by the authority which alone has the appointing power, and for that reason, if for no other, an appointment could not be conferred in the manner suggested. But suppose this were otherwise; suppose the power of appointment to office to reside in the same hand which writes the order for a court-martial, would those mentioned in the order thereby receive appointments to office? If this were so, as Mr. Stanton explained, a *maximum* court martial could not be detailed without making thirteen men hold two offices each, one a military commission of rank as high at least as the rank of the accused, and the other the office of member of the court. If the insertion in the order of the person who is to act as judge advocate is an appointment to office, he too, if a military man, would become the incumbent of two offices. It will be seen that no court martial could legally exist, if the effect of the order detailing its members was as suggested; it would be illegal to order a court at all.

d. It is said, again, that administering the oath to the witnesses implies official position. The difficulty here is that the act of Congress provides otherwise, by providing that the witnesses may be sworn by a judge advocate or "*other person*" who acts as judge advocate.

A foreman of a grand jury is empowered by the statutes of many States to swear witnesses; but did any one ever hear that by doing so he acquired or became invested with an office? The foreman of a grand jury is appointed by the court. If he holds an "office" in the State of New York, at least, there could be no foreman of a grand jury, because the Constitution provides that no power to appoint to office shall reside in a court.

So as to summoning witnesses, the statute provides that the summons shall be made out by the person acting as judge advocate, just as attorneys issue subpœnas and other writs: but does this clothe any one with an "office."

II.

Reference has been made to section 46 of the civil and diplomatic bill of 1852, as if that section and other like statutes had some bearing on the question before us. This section is as follows:

"No person hereafter who holds or shall hold any office under the government of the United States whose salary or annual compensation shall amount to the sum of two thousand five hundred dollars, shall receive compensation for discharging the duties of any other office."

Those familiar with the object and history and settled construction of this and similar provisions, will be puzzled to understand how it can be supposed to have any application to the matter before the committee. The counsel for General Fry frankly states that in his opinion it has no relation to the case, but it is referred to because it was read in the House by the member who connived with General Fry in introducing into the House his libellous letter, or who invoked General Fry's aid in a controversy begun by himself.

1. A representative in Congress is not at all within the words, "*person who holds an office under the government of the United States.*" Senators and representatives do not hold offices *under the government of the United States.* They are part of the government, and therefore are not affected one way or the other by these provisions. (Blount's Trial, U. S. Senate, pp. 22, 102; Wharton's State Trials, pp. 260, 316; 1 Story on the Constitution, §§ 793, 802; Am. Ins. Co. *vs.* Canter, 1 Peters, 511.)

a. Besides, one who, though he has been elected to Congress, has not qualified, holds no office whatever; so that if the position of senator or representative were an "office under the government," even then the present case would not be reached by the statutes in question.

2. Although no such suggestion has been made, let us see whether the provision in question might not be made to apply to the case so far as it would apply if it means that one holding the office of judge advocate could not at the same time be representative elect, and afterwards qualify and receive his salary. We shall see the fallacy of such a construction presently; but let us suppose that the provision applies to the case of one person holding two offices, one of the offices being that of representative elect. Where then shall we land in this case?

a. We are brought up at once by the fact that prosecuting Haddock, just as a judge advocate would have done, does not in any sense constitute holding an "office."

b. But, again, not only is it a fatal trouble with the argument that there was no "office," but the further difficulty must be met that there was no office with "a salary or annual compensation" of twenty-five hundred dollars, or any sum whatever.

Mr. Stanton made an allowance dependent wholly upon the value of the particular service, and graduated in no other way.

3. The greatest difficulty, however, with this and all similar provisions is, that they have no application to any case of two offices actually held at the same time by the same person.

These sections were all enacted to meet an entirely different contingency; and so far as regards any inhibition *they* contain, one person might at once hold all the offices known to the Constitution, from the presidency down. These provisions hit the case of two offices held by separate persons, each drawing pay, and one doing the duties and drawing the pay not only of his own office, *but of the other office also*, while at the same time the incumbent of the second office receives his salary, or is entitled to it. The statute therefore cannot apply to *two offices actually held by the same person*. (Converse *vs.* The United States, 21 How., 463; United States *vs.* Austin (U. S. cir't ct., Mss. Opinion of Cushing, Att'y Gen'l, vol. 8 of Att'y Geul's Op'ns, 325; also opinion of Att'y Gen'l, January 14, 1863; case of General Riley, just decided in Court of Claims; opinion of Bates, Att'y Gen'l, in case of a coroner of District of Columbia.)

III.

Some of the newspaper counsel of General Fry have suggested that, failing in the theory that the act of prosecuting Haddock constituted holding an office, it might be turned into a "contract" with the government, and in that way be made to catch upon a technicality.

The act of 1808 has been cited, and the modest suggestion has been published in a newspaper that the Secretary of War had made a "contract" to have Haddock prosecuted by a representative elect, and for so doing was to be "deemed and taken to be guilty of a high misdemeanor, and be fined in a sum of three thousand dollars!" Those who published this, in the hope of influencing the public or the committee, have, it is submitted, more need to know their place than to know the law; and though it may not be necessary, one or two comments are suggested :

1. The essence of a contract is, that it binds at least two parties. Unless it does this, it does not exist. Did the letter of April 3 constitute any such contract? If the person requested to prosecute Haddock had at any time been unable or unwilling to do so, and the government had thereby suffered loss or inconvenience, could an action for damages have been sustained on the letter of April 3, whether the person so refusing was a member of Congress or not? On the other hand, supposing the government unable like a private party, could an action have been maintained on the letter of April 3, had there been a refusal to allow the party to continue his services?

2. Mr. Stanton and Mr. Dana both testify that no "contract" whatever was made. There was only a request by the Secretary of War, and a written authority to execute that request. The fact that after the service had been rendered the Secretary made a reasonable allowance for it in no way aids the idea that there was any contract.

3. It is no doubt true that a contract might be made between the government and an individual, by which he would be bound on stipulated terms to render professional services, and such a contract might be brought within the letter of the statute, foreign as it would be to its spirit. However that might be, there is no such case here.

4. In this case, moreover, the person was not a member of Congress at the time. The transaction was eight months before he took his seat or qualified as a member of Congress, and for this reason the statute in question has no relation to the case.